GINNY
Off the MAP

GINNY
Off the MAP

Caroline Hickey
Illustrations by Kelly Murphy

Christy Ottaviano Books

LITTLE, BROWN AND COMPANY
New York   Boston

Copyright © 2023 by Caroline Hickey
Illustrations copyright © 2023 by Kelly Murphy

Cover art copyright © 2023 by Kelly Murphy. Cover design by Karina Granda. Cover copyright © 2023 by Hachette Book Group, Inc.
Book design by Elena Aguirre Uranga

Christy Ottaviano Books
Hachette Book Group
1290 Avenue of the Americas, New York, NY 10104
Visit us at LBYR.com

First Edition: June 2023

Christy Ottaviano Books is an imprint of Little, Brown and Company. The Christy Ottaviano Books name and logo are trademarks of Hachette Book Group, Inc.

The publisher is not responsible for websites (or their content) that are not owned by the publisher.

Library of Congress Cataloging-in-Publication Data
Names: Hickey, Caroline, author. | Murphy, Kelly, 1977– illustrator.
Title: Ginny off the map / Caroline Hickey ; illustrations by Kelly Murphy.
Description: First edition. | New York : Little, Brown and Company, 2023. | "Christy Ottaviano Books." | Audience: Ages 8–12. | Summary: "When eleven-year-old Ginny Pierce's father gets deployed to Afghanistan just as her family is moving to a new post in Maryland, she tries to salvage a long and lonely summer by running her own geography camp." —Provided by publisher.
Identifiers: LCCN 2021029223 | ISBN 9780316324625 (hardcover) | ISBN 9780316324823 (ebook)
Subjects: LCSH: Families of military personnel—Juvenile fiction. | Brothers and sisters—Juvenile fiction. | Fathers and daughters—Juvenile fiction. | Interpersonal relations—Juvenile fiction. | Friendship—Juvenile fiction. | CYAC: Children of military personnel—Fiction. | Siblings—Fiction. | Fathers and daughters—Fiction. | Interpersonal relations—Fiction. | Friendship—Fiction.
Classification: LCC PZ7.H5258 My 2007 | DDC 813.6 [Fic]—dc23
LC record available at https://lccn.loc.gov/2021029223

ISBNs: 978-0-316-32462-5 (hardcover), 978-0-316-32482-3 (ebook)

Printed in the United States of America

LSC-C

Printing 1, 2023

For Bridget and Rory
(with a hard hug)

GINNY
Off the MAP

Fact: As you read this, there are approximately twenty volcanoes erupting somewhere in the world.

This is it. The moment I've been dreading.

It's the last day of school and Mr. Sonito is marching down the aisle toward me, his face shiny with sweat. The air-conditioning is broken, and flies buzz in and out through the open windows. Everyone is hot, tired, and ready for the bell to ring.

Basically, our classroom is on the brink of an eruption.

Mr. Sonito stops at my desk, his hand outstretched. I know what he wants.

"Ginny?"

I feign innocence. "Yes?"

"Your science book, please?"

My foot jiggles nervously under my desk. This morning we were told to collect all our textbooks from our lockers and desks and place them in the designated piles at the front of the room. And I did—I returned all of them. Except one.

The Inspiring World of Earth Science is still in my backpack, which is tucked under my desk with my jiggling foot. My copy is old and battered, with rounded corners. The cover is sticky. Inside, it contains chapters on oceanography, hydrology, and atmospheric science. There are project guides detailing how to build a model volcano, how to re-create the formation of Hawaii, and how to make your own power station using the heat that fuels volcanic eruptions.

I love volcanoes. They are the earth literally turning itself inside out.

I don't want to hand in this textbook. I was hoping the last day of school would be so busy that Mr. Sonito would forget all about it and I could keep it.

"I can't find it," I say. "I must have left it at home."

"Really?" Mr. Sonito looks doubtful.

I nod and try to appear apologetic. It's not surprising he doesn't believe me—I never forget my homework or leave books at home. I'm a model student.

"She didn't forget it," Joey Bingle says, twirling a pencil between his fingers. "It's in her backpack. I saw it."

My legs automatically shift to grip my backpack between my knees, and my cheeks flame red. I couldn't look more guilty if I tried.

"Nerd alert!" Joey whisper-shouts. Several kids laugh.

"That's enough, Joey," Mr. Sonito says impatiently. He wipes his brow with the back of his hand. "The book, please, Ginny."

I retrieve the book and hand it over. As Mr. Sonito walks it to the correct pile at the front of the room, I glare at Joey. He smirks back at me, looking triumphant.

Even though our school is a STEM-themed magnet, which means kids have to take a placement test to go here and we spend more time on science and math than the average school, my intellectual aptitude and intense love of geography still make me a bit of an outlier.

Well, a major outlier.

"Thanks a lot," I mutter to Joey under my breath.

"Anytime," he replies.

Eventually, the last bell rings and we're dismissed. Joey gives me a cheeky wave as he runs out the door. I consider going up to Mr. Sonito to apologize, but he's deep in conversation with Lily and Emma, who are wearing their hair in matching high ponytails. They remind me of the twin cities of Minneapolis and St. Paul: originally separate entities, but over time they've pretty much merged into one.

As I check my locker for stray pencils and erasers, kids alternate between exchanging goodbyes and shouting things like, "We're free!" and "Have a great summer!"

I follow the stream of kids out of the building, listening as they plan pool parties and sleepovers and other first-day-of-summer activities. I'm about to board the steps of my bus when a horn honks sharply. I look up and see my parents' car parked at the curb. Mom's arm is out the window, waving at me.

I hurry over to the car. "What are you doing here?" I ask. "You didn't tell me you were picking me up."

Mom gestures for me to get in. "Your dad and I thought it'd be a fun surprise to take you girls out for ice cream to celebrate the last day of school."

That's odd. Mom isn't the "fun surprise" type. She's the "if it isn't on the calendar then it isn't happening" type.

I open the back door and slide in next to my sister, Allie. She's sulking and holding a basketball in her lap.

"What's wrong?" I ask her.

"Nothing," she says. "Just that I was planning to go to Mara's after school. Most of my team is meeting up there and then going swimming at Avery's."

Allie's basketball team is her life. She plays shooting guard, and every time we go to her games someone says to me, *Your sister is amazing! Can you shoot like that too?*

Short answer: No.

"Can you meet them at Avery's when we're done?" I ask her.

"I don't know. Hopefully." She side-eyes our parents, then looks out the window.

"How was the last day of fifth grade, Ginny?" Dad asks.

"Frustrating. We didn't learn anything, and I had to hand in my science book, which I really wanted to keep."

I can always be myself with Dad. He's one of the few people who understands me.

"You're not *supposed* to learn anything on the last day," Allie says. "School's over."

My sister is twelve and a half. I'm eleven. Despite being just one grade apart, we have very little in common besides our shared DNA, which for full siblings is only about 50 percent.

"I like learning," I remind her. "How else am I going to make an important geographic discovery one day like Marie Tharp?"

Marie Tharp is my hero. She made the first map of the Atlantic Ocean floor and proved the theory of continental drift.

"Yeah, yeah," Allie says, rolling her eyes. "I know all about your big plan to be famous."

She's wrong—I don't care about being famous. I just want to make a significant contribution to our knowledge of Earth. Anyway, what's wrong with having plans? Allie has plans too. It's just that hers involve hanging out with her friends and improving her shooting accuracy by practicing one-armed shots.

Which is perfectly fine, by the way. It's just not what *I* like doing.

Dad drives us to the Utterly Delicious Creamery, our favorite ice cream parlor in Fayetteville. He pulls into the parking lot, and we all get out of the car and head to the walk-up window. We place our order and sit down at one of the picnic tables nearby to wait.

"I'm really going to miss the homemade ice cream here," Dad says.

"Me too," I agree.

"I doubt they'll have a place like this in Maryland," Allie says sadly.

"You're right," Mom says. "They probably won't have any ice cream at all. Just vegetables. And bran. And maybe some really stale fruitcakes."

"Ha, ha," Allie replies. "I just meant that I'm going to miss North Carolina, and Tar Heels games, and going to Duck in the summer..."

We've been stationed here for two years, with Dad working as an ER doctor at the Womack Army Medical Center. He got new orders in April and is being transferred to Walter Reed National Military Medical Center, in Maryland. We move in eight days.

"Don't worry, Allie Cat," says Dad. "Our new house is only twenty minutes from the University of Maryland! We can go to all the Terps games. And Maryland has great beaches. You'll love Ocean City."

"I'll never be a Terps fan. I'm a Tar Heel." She sighs heavily.

This will be our fifth move since I was born. I know

it's probably good practice for all the travel I'll do as a geoscientist one day, but this move feels especially difficult. I was just starting to get settled here and know my way around and now—boom! We're off again.

Allie starts dribbling her basketball, its rhythm getting faster and faster. If basketballs could sound annoyed, hers would.

Dad says, "Allie, please?"

She sighs and catches the ball, then places it between her ankles. One of the servers brings us our order.

Dad raises his cone in a toast. Mom and I do the same, but Allie hesitates. Dad looks at her expectantly until she lifts her cone with ours.

"To our family," Dad says, "and our next adventure!"

The four of us clink cones and dig in. I got a double scoop of birthday cake with extra sprinkles on top, so I eat mine slowly, savoring the crunchy sprinkles.

Dad finishes his cone first because he bites instead of licks his ice cream. When he's done, his feet start tapping, and then the fingers on his left hand start drumming. It's very unlike him.

"Dad? Are you okay?" I ask.

He stops immediately. "Of course."

I don't believe him. He's an ER doctor. He's always calm, steady, and in command. He doesn't fidget.

Allie finishes her cone, crumples her napkin, and fires it into the trash can five feet away.

"Nice shot, Allie Cat," Dad says.

She exhales dramatically. "We've had our ice cream. So go on, tell us. What is it?"

The hairs on the back of my neck prick up. Allie senses it too. Something's definitely going on.

"What do you mean, 'what is it'?" Mom asks, rotating her cone to look for drips. She still has more than half of her butter pecan left because she eats so neatly.

"You wouldn't have picked me and Ginny up and made me skip going to Mara's for no reason," Allie says. "So tell us what's wrong."

Dad and Mom exchange a look, and both of their faces twitch. Now *all* the hairs on my body are pricking up and I've got goose bumps on my arms. I've read about this—it's caused by the body's subconscious release of adrenaline. In animals, it helps prepare for a fight-or-flight reaction, while in humans it happens when we're afraid, under stress, or feeling strong emotions.

Right now, I'm all three.

After what feels like an eon, Dad says, "I got some news yesterday. The doctor I was supposed to split my next deployment with was just placed on medical leave. So now, instead of me deploying in early 2015, I'm taking his turn and doing the first half of the tour."

I feel my stomach flip. Maybe the earth flips too. All the ice cream that was in my stomach is now up in my throat.

"That's not fair," I say. "We're in the middle of transferring to a new station—you can't get deployed at the same time!"

Mom jumps in, her voice as buttery and smooth as her ice cream. "It is an unusual situation, Ginny. But you know how quickly things can change. And sometimes doctors are assigned randomly to units. We're lucky your dad is still able to split the deployment and won't be going for the whole time."

"Where are you going?" Allie asks Dad.

"Same as the original plan," he replies. "Afghanistan. I leave next Friday for two weeks of training in California, and then I deploy for six months. I should be back around Christmas."

Leave next Friday?

Back around Christmas?

10

My stomach flips again, and I feel sick. I hope I don't throw up in the parking lot of the Utterly Delicious. That would be utterly disgusting.

"But what about our summer plans?" I ask. "Going to the headquarters of the Society of Woman Geographers? Doing all the Smithsonian museums together? Visiting Calvert Cliffs?" I can hear my voice getting shrill on that last one, but I can't help it. It's the most well-known fossil site on the East Coast, and I've always wanted to go.

"I'm sorry," Dad says. "Believe me, I'm disappointed too."

"Postpone it," I plead. "Get someone else to take your place. *Please.*"

Mom interjects. "I know this is tough news, but I promise, it's going to be just fi—"

Allie pounds the table with her fist, then jumps up and storms off, disappearing around the corner of the ice cream parlor.

Allie and I don't agree on much, but seeing her upset makes me feel even worse. Hot, silent tears start pouring down my cheeks.

I can't tell if I'm more sad or more angry. I think angry. Angry at this news, and angry that this is our life.

I didn't choose it. I try my best to go along with it and be a resilient military kid, but sometimes enough is enough.

I start to hiccup and can't stop. The hiccups get louder and louder. I definitely should not have gotten a double scoop.

Dad goes to the ice cream parlor window and comes back with a bottle of water and a stack of napkins. He unscrews the cap on the water bottle and holds it out to me.

"Ginny," he says in a low voice, "do you want a sip of this?"

I nod and accept the water bottle. I take a few small sips and hand it back to him. A minute later, the hiccups stop.

Dad hands me the napkins to clean myself up.

I make a half-hearted effort to dry my tears and wipe my nose, but I don't really care what I look like. We're leaving North Carolina in a few days. So what if some kids from school see me sobbing at the Utterly Delicious?

They'd sob too, if they were me.

Mom gets up and says, "I'm going to check on Allie."

Dad and I sit quietly for a few minutes. Then I say, "Dad, we can't move to Maryland without you. We just can't! I need you."

"I know," he says. He takes off his glasses and puts them on the table. He rubs his face with both hands. When he stops, I see that his eyes are bloodshot. Were they like that earlier and I didn't notice?

He clears his throat. "Listen, you know Mom and I will do everything we can think of to help you and Allie with this move. We've already applied to another STEM school there for you, and we found a house in a neighborhood with a lot of kids your age. The only difference now is that I won't be joining you for the first few months."

"*Six* months," I correct him. "Six long, painful months."

"It'll go fast. It'll be okay."

"No, it won't. It *won't*."

Dad grabs my hand and holds it. "Let's take a break and talk about something else for a minute. I saw an article yesterday about Mount Vesuvius. What do you know about it?"

"Mount Vesuvius?" My fact brain snaps to attention. "I know it's one of the world's most dangerous volcanoes, that it's located in southern Italy, and that its infamous eruption in 79 CE buried the town of Pompeii and killed at least a thousand people."

Dad nods appreciatively. "Why am I not surprised you know all that?"

I beam. I can't help it. I love trading facts with Dad.

"But," he goes on, "did you know that during that eruption, it spewed over 1.5 million tons of hot ash and rock *per second*? That's the equivalent of shooting out 250,000 fully grown elephants every single second."

I picture it—a quarter of a million elephants shooting up out of a volcano every second. How would they fit coming out of the top? Would they cover the sky completely? Where would they land, and how high would they pile up?

Would their faces look surprised?

Now I can't stop thinking about millions of elephants flying through the air. I see them blotting out the sky, their legs splayed, trunks curled high.

"You're imagining the elephants, aren't you?" Dad says.

I nod. "How'd you know?"

He smiles. "Because that's what I did when I read it. I kept thinking about and seeing elephants for days."

I lean closer to him and rest my head against his shoulder. Dad is the one person who really, truly gets me. Most people think I'm too nerdy, too intense. Even in my own family. Mom and Allie don't say it, but I'm pretty sure they think it.

But to Dad, I'm just right. I'm elephants flying through the sky—a wonder.

2

Fact: Almost everyone has a skewed perception of the true size of countries due to a cartographic technique called the Mercator projection, which exaggerates the size of landmasses near the poles while diminishing areas near the equator. Commonly used in textbooks, on classroom maps, and even on Google Maps, it drastically reduces the size of Africa, India, China, and South America, while inflating North America and Greenland.

Within a week, we've boxed up and labeled nearly everything in our Fayetteville house. The military is supposed to take care of packing and moving for us, but Mom is so particular that she insists on us doing it ourselves.

I don't mind packing, generally. I like being organized and knowing exactly where all my things are. But this time, we're packing up to leave Dad, not just Fayetteville. I feel like I'm the *Titanic*, and every box is an iceberg. I move so slowly that Mom eventually barges into my room and packs it all up for me.

She's gone out to get more packing tape when Dad finds me sitting at the kitchen table writing out geography facts on index cards. I keep them in a green plastic file box. Some of the facts I'm writing I've already memorized, but I like having them stored all in one place, in case I need them for a future paper or project.

"Ginny, can you help me in the garage?" Dad asks. "I've got a lot more to do, and I want to finish before Mom gets back and makes me throw everything out."

I don't want to pack anymore, but I say yes because the extra time alone with Dad is worth it.

I follow him into the garage, where a talk radio program is discussing the week's health-care news. Dad loves talk radio, and we always listen to it when we're working on projects together. We'd talked about building a 3D map of Washington, DC, this summer. Just one more thing we won't get to do now that he's being deployed sooner.

"What are they talking about today?" I ask.

"This and that. Mostly heart disease."

"Oh. Fun."

He grins. "You know me—I listen to whatever might be useful. Life is short, so you may as well learn all you can."

It's such a Dad thing to say, something he's probably said to me a zillion times before. Yet it feels like a box cutter plunging into my heart.

I look at him sadly, already missing him.

"Hey, now." He hands me a flat box and tape. "Don't waste your tears on me yet, Ginny. I still need your manual labor. Tape this up for me?"

I grab the box and start folding it into shape. Then I carefully tape up its seams. Dad takes it from me, writes *Garage—Tools* on the side, and draws a smiley face wearing glasses on it.

"A smile makes everything easier," he says. "I was thinking this morning that I'll really miss Fayetteville. How about you?"

"Me too. I love this house and I liked my school pretty well and I'll miss Adam and Shuri."

With every move, I leave behind a friend or two I really like. And Adam and Shuri have been particularly good ones. They're both easy to get along with and enjoy discussing interesting things, like the giant permafrost explosions in Siberia. We'll keep in touch, but I already know that most friendships don't survive living several states apart.

"I'm going to miss you the most," I tell him. "Can't you *try* to find a way to delay your deployment? Switch with someone else?"

I'd rather give up an arm than have Dad leave in two days. Just not my right arm because I'm right-handed. Or my left, because I might need it for carrying water and my camera when he and I hike the trail to Machu Picchu the summer after I graduate high school. Machu Picchu is an ancient Incan city in Peru that's made entirely of stone and located on top of a mountain. It's been designated one of the New Seven Wonders of the World.

On second thought, maybe I wouldn't rather give up an arm. I'd give up just about anything else, though.

"I can't delay my deployment or our transfer to Maryland because the orders have already been cut," Dad reminds me. He wads up sheets of newspaper to layer in the bottom of the box, then wraps his tool kit in a length of bubble wrap. "But I do have some good news I've been waiting to tell you."

I don't reply, doubtful there could be any news that would feel good right now. Being a military family is always hard, but you very rarely get a transfer and a deployment at the same time. They're on different cycles for a reason.

Resigned, I pick up another box and start folding it.

"Do you want to hear the good news?" Dad asks.

"I guess."

He smiles. "I found an amazing camp for you in Maryland."

"Camp?" I flash back to some of the day camps Allie and I have gone to over the years. They were mostly crafts for me, sports for her. I made a lot of face masks with paper plates and Popsicle sticks and watched other kids have aggressive squirt-gun fights. These camps were so boring it was like watching paint dry. In fact, at one of those camps it was *literally* that. The art counselor wouldn't let me leave her area until my paper-plate mask passed the fingertip test.

I scowl.

"Listen before you say no," Dad says. "This camp is different. It's a geography camp! It's three weeks long and includes cartography, building digital interactive maps, and an outdoor geocaching challenge."

"Seriously?" My voice goes up an octave. I've never heard of a camp like this.

21

Dad nods. "Yep. I think you'll love it."

I picture myself having long conversations debating the advantages and disadvantages of the Mercator projection and how maps shape our understanding of the world. To be in a room with other future geographers? It's a dream come true.

I throw my arms around Dad. "Thank you! It sounds perfect!"

Dad squeezes me hard. His hugs are always bear hugs. "You're welcome, Ginny. I hope it helps."

We're still mid-hug when Allie walks in, wearing her favorite Tar Heels T-shirt. She must have just gotten home.

She scoops up a nearby soccer ball, bounces it three times, then tosses it into the long, netted sleeve with a rim at the top that we use for storing balls.

"Very nice!" Dad says. "You're doing much better with your wrist snap."

Allie shrugs, as if the shot was too easy to bother celebrating. But I know she's pleased Dad noticed her wrist. She's been in the driveway working on it for weeks.

"Do you want to help us pack?" he asks her.

"Not really," she replies. "But I will." She grabs a flat cardboard box and starts to fold it into shape, then snatches the tape from my hand. She moves quickly, gathering up Nerf guns, a Wiffle bat, and a ring toss game that no one plays anymore.

"Allie, guess what?" I say.

"What?"

"Dad signed me up for a special geography camp near our new house. It's got cartography and geocaching!"

"Hmm. Cool."

"We signed you up for a basketball camp in August, Allie," Dad says.

"I know." Allie throws a pair of inline skates and several lacrosse balls into the box. "Mom already told me. Thanks."

Her voice is flat and tense. She usually sounds more like the happy, carefree kids on commercials, who joke around a lot and heat up waffles in the toaster after school. She's been a full-on drama queen since Dad told us about the deployment, acting like it's only happening to her.

"Why are *you* upset?" I ask her. "As soon as we move to Maryland, you'll go outside with your basketball and come back an hour later with a new best friend."

Allie looks at me with disdain. "Just leave me alone, Ginny, okay? You may be a genius, but you don't know everything."

I've never said I know everything. In fact, the smarter a person is, the more aware they are of how much they still have to learn.

I look at Dad to mediate the situation, but instead of saying something to smooth things over, Dad nods toward the door, indicating he wants me to give him and Allie some privacy.

"Why do *I* have to leave?" I protest. "I was here first."

Dad stares back at me, his expression firm. I know he wants me to bow out gracefully.

I feel myself getting angry at my sister. Really super-duper, over-the-top angry. But having a big fight with Dad here when we have such little time left together would be dumb. So instead I huff a few times and stomp out of the garage.

In my room full of boxes, there's nothing to do. All of my books and art supplies are packed. Frustrated, I kick one of the smaller cartons, then flop on my bed.

Allie and I see the world differently. I think I'm right, and she thinks she's right. It's like with Mercator projection maps—people who are used to them have a hard time believing that the shortest way to fly from

Washington, DC, to Shanghai, China, is to go up and over the North Pole, rather than fly west.

I guess when you've been looking at something one way for a long time, it's really hard to see it any other way.

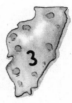

Fact: A fully developed avalanche can travel at a speed of over two hundred miles per hour and weigh as much as a million tons.

It's Dad's last night at home.

Dinner is late because we're still packing, but Mom makes everyone's favorite—tacos. I set the table, and Allie pours the drinks. We're using paper plates and cups since our kitchen stuff is in boxes. Mom cuts up a bunch of green onions, Dad's favorite, and puts them by his plate.

I feel like I'm watching everything in slow motion, even myself. Like I'm outside my body, which is placing forks on the left and folding napkins so the sides line up. It can't be me sitting down for my last dinner with my dad for six long months.

Dad deployed to Iraq when I was in first grade, so I've been through this before, but it feels so different this time. Now I know what's going on and how long half a year is.

Dad sits at the head of the table wearing a paper crown I made for him on Father's Day when I was eight. It says *#1 Dad* and has heart stickers on it.

"I didn't know you still had that," I tell him.

Dad adjusts it carefully, as if it were made of gold. "I keep all the things you and Allie make me."

Mom puts a paper plate of taco meat in the middle of the table along with tortillas and those crunchy stand-up taco bowls. We start eating. Not having our regular plates and silverware shouldn't matter, but it does. It feels fake. It doesn't feel like a real family dinner.

Everyone is quiet. Normally we talk about Mom's work projects or Dad's day at the hospital or Allie's latest game or whatever I'm reading about at the moment.

Allie plays with her food more than eats it. "Connor's family went to their favorite restaurant and ordered huge steaks and hot fudge sundaes the night before his dad deployed last year," she says.

I kick her under the table. Her tone makes it clear she thinks Connor's family's last-night-together dinner was better than ours. Why would she do that?

Allie kicks me back, harder. She continues, "Then they went to the batting cages and hit balls and rode go-karts."

Luckily, Dad doesn't take the bait. "That sounds fun," he says. "But I'd rather be at home with you guys, wearing my Sunday pants."

Dad's Sunday pants are an old pair of navy-blue sweatpants with an elastic waist. Whenever he gets home from a shift at the hospital, he puts them on, no matter what day of the week it is.

"This house isn't our home anymore," Allie replies. "It's all packed up."

Mom frowns. "*Allie.* Please don't make this more difficult than it already is."

"It's okay," Dad says. "She's allowed to be upset."

Allie jabs at the taco meat to load more into her shell. Her plastic fork snaps in half, and the bottom half falls into the meat.

Mom gets up and grabs another fork for her. Allie's face is red and furious. I don't blame her—that's how I feel too. But I don't want Dad's last night here with us ruined. I want this dinner to be a happy memory.

I have to fix this.

"You want to hear something amazing?" I blurt out. "The Appalachian Mountains are shrinking. They used to be as tall as the Himalayas, but over millions of years, constant wind and rain have caused them to erode."

Allie groans. "So what? Who even cares?"

"Allie, *enough!*" Mom says.

"Sorry," Allie replies. "I'm just not interested in acting like everything is fine. And I'm *definitely* not interested in random mountain facts that don't have anything to do with what we're talking about."

I know she's right, but I also know that Mom and Dad are sitting here pretending this isn't the hardest, most awful dinner ever and I had to say *something*.

Instead of just explaining that, however, I snap back at my sister.

"My fact wasn't random." My insides feel like they're burning, like I've swallowed hot sauce. Talking seems like the only way to make the pain stop. "We're in North Carolina, and we're moving to Maryland. The Appalachian Mountains run through both states. They're almost two thousand miles long, stretching from Alabama up into Canada."

"You can't be serious," Allie says, disgusted. "That's what you're thinking about right now? What is wrong with you?"

"Girls, please," Dad interjects. He sounds old and tired—not like himself. "Can we just have a pleasant final dinner together?"

"*Final*?" Allie repeats. "Nice word choice."

Dad looks at me helplessly. Even though I feel the same way Allie does, my allegiance is to him.

"Don't be such a jerk," I tell her.

"No name-calling," Mom scolds.

Allie narrows her eyes, ready to spit back an insult, when Mom cuts in again.

"Anyone want more cheese?" She shoves her chair back hard and gets up to root around in the fridge. She comes back with two slices of American. "There's no more shredded cheese, but we might as well use these up."

The slices have that old, whitish look to them, like they're just about to start growing mold. Allie shakes her head. I do too—I've lost my appetite. There's something really pathetic about eating moldy cheese on our last night together.

"I'll take them, Liz." Dad messes with his taco for a minute, stuffing in the cheese slices. Then he says, "What do you all think about a family trip at Christmas break when I'm back? We could go skiing for a few days. There are some ski resorts not too far from our new house."

He mostly looks at Allie as he says this.

"Yeah, okay," she says grudgingly. "I would like to go skiing."

"Great idea," Mom says. She's smiling, but her eyes look wet and shiny. "A ski trip would be a good thing to look forward to."

"I don't know how to ski," I remind everyone. Allie went a few times when we lived in Tacoma, but I've never gone. "Can't we do something else?"

"So take a *lesson*," Allie says, exasperated. "How do you think everyone else learns?"

I glare back at her. "*Or* we could do something everyone likes. We've always talked about going to New York."

"That's a great idea too," Dad agrees.

"Sure—side with Ginny. You always do." Allie shoves her chair back and carries her plate to the trash can. "I'm going upstairs to call Mara."

The hot-sauce feeling in my stomach rises up in my throat. There's so much going wrong in our family right now.

I take a slow, deep breath to calm myself. But I do it at the same time as I bite into my taco. I inhale too sharply and start choking on a wad of tortilla and meat.

I panic. My eyes water. I pound on the table to get Dad's attention.

"Ginny?" he says. "Are you okay?"

I shake my head urgently and point at my throat.

Dad immediately jumps behind me, wraps his arms around my chest, and pushes into my ribs with his fist until I spit out the meat. At the same time, my chest lunges forward, hitting the edge of my plate that's hanging over the table, and tilting it down so that my food falls in my lap. Warm taco splatters all over my thighs.

It's not hot enough to burn me, but I let out a cry like I've been scalded. It's the sound of everything I've been holding in.

Mom grabs the paper towels and hands them to me. I start patting my lap, and Dad puts his hands on my shoulders.

"That wasn't like you," he says.

"I know," I say quietly. "I'm—"

But I can't finish the sentence. I don't have the words. And I'm not like Allie, who can yell and make a scene and storm off and show everyone exactly how she's feeling.

I hold my feelings in. And choke on them, apparently.

He sighs. "It's going to be okay, Ginny," he says. "I know everything seems bad right now, but we'll get through this."

I nod as I blot myself dry. But he knows and I know that it won't be "we" getting through this.

That's the problem.

))⟩ ———— ⟨((

After dinner is cleaned up, Dad says to Mom, "Why don't you go see what Allie is up to, and Ginny and I will go for a walk?"

Mom nods her okay, and Dad looks at me expectantly. My shorts are wet from the spill, but I don't want to miss a minute with Dad, so I decide not to change them and follow him outside.

The houses are all spread out in this neighborhood and there aren't many streetlights, so you can see a lot of stars.

"Little Dipper, Big Dipper," Dad says, pointing.

33

My turn. "Lyra."

"Cassiopeia."

"Draco and Hercules."

"Very good," Dad says.

I start to forget about my damp shorts. It's a perfect summer evening, warm with a light breeze. The air smells like flowers in bloom. How can the world be so beautiful and at the same time feel like it's ending?

"Tomorrow will be a very hard day," Dad says. He takes my hand and holds it. We're walking side by side, and it's dark enough that I can't see his face well.

"Yeah."

"While I'm gone, I want you and Allie to lean on each other," Dad says. "You need to be a team."

"Allie doesn't want me to lean on her."

"That's not true."

"She wishes I could be more *like* her," I explain, "but that's not the same thing."

It's a full minute before Dad answers me. "Allie is your older sister. She's always going to look out for you, no matter what."

"Yeah, maybe. It's just that new schools, new people—all that stuff is much easier for her. We're going to get to Maryland and Allie will have five new friends in five minutes and try out for a basketball team and get elected captain, all before the first week is over. And I'll just be, you know, *me*."

Dad laughs. "I like 'you.'"

I like me too. But I'm not the kid everyone wants to be best friends with. I'm the kid they ask to help them with their homework.

"Listen," Dad says. "While I'm away, Ginny, I need you to be the glue. I need you to stay positive and keep everyone together, even when it's hard."

"Me? Why not Mom or Allie?"

Dad nudges me with his elbow. "Because I know you can do it, that's why."

I'm not sure that's true but I nod, because I want Dad to be proud of me. I want him to think I can do this— that I can be the glue.

Dad stops walking and positions us just under a streetlight. "I have a present for you," he says, pulling something silver and shiny out of his pocket and handing it to me.

It looks like the fancy makeup compact Mom uses for special occasions. When I press the button on one side, the cover pops open, and I see that it's a compass.

It's beautiful. "Thank you, Dad. I love it!"

"Turn it over," he says.

I turn it over and engraved on the back are the words *Follow your true north.*

Nearby there's a mailbox encased in stone with a flat top. I place the compass on it and watch as the needle trembles and twitches its way around the face, then finally points back in the direction of our house.

"There's north," I say.

"True north?" Dad asks.

"Well, no, of course not."

"Because why?" He's playing our game, where he tests me by pretending not to know something I know he knows.

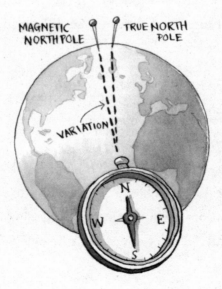

"Because the earth is a giant magnet, so a compass's needle points to the *magnetic* North Pole. True north is the *geographic* North Pole, which means it's at the top of the world where the lines of longitude converge."

"So they're not the same?" Dad asks.

"They can't be. The magnetic North Pole is always moving and shifting because of the earth's molten core. It used to be in the Canadian Arctic, but now it's steadily moving toward Siberia at a rate of thirty-four miles per year."

"That's my girl." Dad's face breaks into a huge smile. "Do you understand what the engraving means?"

I think it over. Why would Dad tell me to follow *my* true north? "No. What does it mean?"

"It's a concept," he says. "When people talk about finding their 'true north,' what they mean is finding their own path or purpose in life. Sort of like their own internal compass that will guide them."

I imagine a compass located somewhere in my abdomen, its needle pointing me in the right direction.

"While I'm gone, Ginny, I want you to remember to follow *your* true north and be yourself, even if it's hard sometimes."

"How can I not be myself? Who else would I be?"

Dad takes my hand again. "It might not make sense right now. But hold the idea in your mind. When I come back, you can explain it to me."

I shake my head. "I don't get it, Dad."

"You will. Just follow where your compass is pointing, Ginny. Your compass, not anyone else's."

Fact: The United States is home to some pretty unusual place names, including Monkey's Eyebrow, Kentucky; Booger Hole, West Virginia; Hot Coffee, Mississippi; Boring, Oregon; and No Name, Colorado.

I'm in my new room in Silver Spring, Maryland, unpacking my last box. It's mostly books and some board games. I take my time arranging everything on my bookshelf, grouping the books by subject and then alphabetizing them by the author's last name.

When I get to the bottom of the box, I see a flat package wrapped in brown paper. The words *Open Me* are scrawled in black marker in Dad's handwriting. I tear open the paper and find a huge, hardcover book about Afghanistan, with photographs and data and maps. It weighs several pounds.

I clutch it excitedly to my chest. It's been two weeks since Dad left, and this is exactly what I need to distract myself. I flip to the map section in the middle and immediately grab a piece of posterboard and my colored pencils so I can make my own version. Working on it will be almost like being with Dad.

Right now, he's on a plane flying from his training camp in California to Fort Benning, Georgia, then to England, then to Cyprus, and then on to Afghanistan. Before you go into a war zone, you first transfer to a military base, which is why there are so many stops. I've marked all of them on my world wall map with pushpins.

I sketch the border of Afghanistan, then pencil in Kabul, which is both the capital and largest city. It's at least 3,500 years old and one of the ancient world's most developed cities.

There's a sharp knock on my door. Without waiting for an answer, Allie barges in. It startles me so much that my hand jumps, my pencil dragging a long, errant line down my map.

I grab my eraser to fix the mistake. "Allie! You're supposed to knock and then *wait* to be invited in."

"Sorry." Allie's eating cashews, picking them out of a bag in one hand and popping them in her mouth. "What are you doing?"

I shuffle my colored pencils so they're in rainbow order. "Making a relief map of Afghanistan."

"That's a *relief*," she jokes. "I thought you might be doing something boring, like studying."

"Ha, ha. A relief map uses color and texture to show the elevations and depressions in the land," I explain.

"Yeah, yeah, I know." She digs for another cashew as her eyes survey my bedroom, its walls already covered in my handmade maps. "Your room is like being inside a giant geography textbook."

"Thanks."

"It wasn't a compliment."

I don't respond, and she continues to linger in my doorway. I wonder if she wants something.

"The kids on the street are getting ready to play manhunt," she says.

Manhunt is like hide-and-seek in reverse, where one person or group hides and everyone else has to find them. Allie loves outdoor games. All games, really, that involve running, hiding, and tagging people. Dad says she has more energy than the average person and needs a way to get it out, but I think she just likes winning at things.

"Have fun." I continue drawing contour lines. I love contour lines; I think they're beautiful.

"Why don't you come out with us? You haven't even met anyone here yet."

"No, thanks."

Allie eyes the new book from Dad. "You can't stay in your room reading for the next six months."

"I won't. My camp starts in a few days."

BANG! Bang! BANG!

Annoyed, I clap my hands over my ears. "What's that?"

"I think Mom's hanging something." Allie taps her foot impatiently. "Come outside with me. Just to meet everybody."

"Why do you keep asking? You've barely talked to me in days." A thought pops into my head. "Did Dad tell you to help me make friends here or something?"

Allie's cheeks flush. I've guessed right.

"Oh, forget it," she says. She turns and leaves, shutting my door hard behind her. I hear her feet thunder down the stairs.

The hammering starts up again, louder than before.

I wish Mom would calm down. She's in full Military Mom mode and hasn't stopped working since we got to Maryland. She had us unpacked in just two days and immediately began hanging pictures and curtains and filling the pantry. She even painted the upstairs bathroom.

The weird thing is, there's none of Dad's stuff anywhere. She hung up his clothes in his closet, but there's nothing of his around the house. In Fayetteville, his sneakers were by the door; his baseball cap was on the coat closet doorknob; and his copies of *Scientific American* were always lying around. We don't even have his favorite bacon in the fridge here because Mom doesn't like how much mess it makes to cook it.

Instead of feeling like he's deployed, it feels like he's been erased from our lives.

I pick up a brown colored pencil to shade in some lower ground on my map and press down so hard that the tip breaks off.

BANG! Bang! BANG!

I can't focus on my map with all the banging. I want to finish it quickly and send a picture to Dad so he knows how much I love the book he gave me. I want to show him that I'm trying to stay positive and be the glue.

I get up and head down the stairs, only making it halfway before I find Mom. She's hammering nails into the wall of the first-floor hallway in a straight line, one after another.

BANG! Bang!

"Mom, I'm making a map," I say.

"That's nice," she mumbles, a nail between her teeth. "Of what?"

"Of Afghanistan. Do you have to hang pictures right now?"

"I'm not hanging pictures," she says. "I'm hanging hooks because this house doesn't have a mudroom."

She nods toward her favorite wooden sign leaning against the wall: *A place for everything and everything in its place.* Dad bought it for her at a flea market a few years ago because it reminded him so much of her.

Mom lines up another nail, gives it a light tap to start the hole, then a much harder *BANG!* to drive it through.

Tap BANG!

"Sorry," she says. "I'm almost done, I promise. Why don't you go outside and play with Allie and the neighbors while I finish?"

"No, thanks. I really want to work on my map."

"There's more to life than geography, Ginny."

"Not to me."

Mom sighs. "Well, it would be good to meet a few people here before school starts. And Allie says they're all really nice."

I don't answer. I have no doubt the kids are nice. Maybe they're even really smart and really fun and a million other great things. But that doesn't mean I'll enjoy playing manhunt with them more than I'm enjoying drawing this map. And it's my summer, and my time. I want to use it to do things I like.

Out of nowhere, a memory from Dad's last deployment pops into my head.

"Do you know where our Flat Daddy is?"

Mom looks surprised. "You remember that?"

I don't remember too much from last time, because I was only six, but I definitely remember our Flat Daddy. It was a life-sized cardboard version of Dad. A lot of military families have them made when their loved one is deployed. Especially if they have little kids.

Mom used to position ours sitting at the kitchen table with Allie and me, or have it lounging on a chair in the TV room. Sometimes we took pictures with it and emailed them to Dad. Allie used to pretend it was really Dad and talk to it.

"Of course I remember it," I say. "Where is it?"

Mom drops the nail she was holding in her mouth and bends over, searching the floor with her fingertips. When she stands up, she looks guilty.

"I thought you and Allie had gotten too old for it," she says. "I got rid of it a few years ago when we moved from Washington to North Carolina."

Mom got rid of our Flat Daddy? That belonged to me and Allie, not her. It was a gift from our grandparents.

I feel suddenly hot, as if I've just stepped into the Sahara desert. "Does Allie know?"

"I'm not sure. She hasn't asked about it." Mom looks at me apologetically. "I'm sorry, Ginny. I didn't realize it meant that much to you."

I stare at Mom for another minute, biting back all the things I want to say to her.

Allie and I get moved around every few years like we're chess pieces, and she can't even *ask* before she throws out our things? If Mom didn't know whether we wanted it or not, she should have asked us. That's what Dad would have done.

"It's fine," I say finally, not meaning it one little bit. Then I turn and march back up the steps and into my room. Mom goes right back to hammering as if nothing happened.

Tap BANG! BANG! BANG!

I shut my door firmly. I grab my tablet and earbuds, hoping I can find something good to listen to online while I work on my map. But then I hear another sound—kids shouting. I go to my window and push it open, letting in the steamy summer air.

I poke my head out to see what's going on. Our new house is on a cul-de-sac called Curtis Court, and the kids here play games right in the street because there's no through traffic. Two boys taller than Allie have tagged her and appear to be dragging her off to jail. A little girl who's probably five or six is giggling and pointing as Allie makes a silly face at her. I see another boy hiding in a honeysuckle bush, apparently not found yet.

Allie looks happy. She looks like she's lived here forever, not like a new kid who moved in two weeks ago. She hasn't even mentioned Mara, and they were inseparable in Fayetteville. How does she do it?

There's more laughing and shouting from outside. I shut the window and put in my earbuds, cueing up a playlist on the tablet. It's 6:10 PM, or 1810, military

47

time, which means Dad's plane has been in the air for an hour already. By tomorrow night, he should have arrived safely, likely at Bagram Airfield, which is the largest US military base in Afghanistan and resides at an elevation of 4,895 feet.

I sit back down with my map and take a few deep breaths. I turn my sky-blue colored pencil over and over in my pencil sharpener, watching the shavings collect in a little pile. Even though the music and breathing are helping, there's still an anxious, agitated feeling in the pit of my stomach. Is it because Dad is on the plane and I'm worried about him?

Or because I'm sitting alone in a room in Silver Spring, Maryland, missing everything about our old life?

I mentally list some of the most depressing town names in the United States. Cape Disappointment, Washington. Dismal, North Carolina. Misery Bay, Michigan.

If I had to guess, I'd say they were all named by military kids who had recently moved.

Fact: One of the longest place names in the world is a hill in New Zealand called Taumatawhakatangihangakoauauotamatea-turipukakapikimaungahoronukupokaiwhen-uakitanatahu, which is eighty-five letters and basically means "the place where Tamatea, the man with the big knees, who slid, climbed, and swallowed mountains, known as 'landeater,' played his flute to his loved one."

I'm so excited for camp I could hardly sleep. This will be my first time doing geocaching, which is like a giant treasure-hunting game where you use GPS to seek out containers people have filled with items and hidden in random locations. Dad and I have talked about doing it together—we just hadn't gotten around to it.

I dress carefully, because I want to be ready for anything. I wear my hiking shoes and pith helmet, then slip my compass, a pencil, and a few index cards in the pocket of my cargo shorts. The pith helmet is probably too much, but where else am I going to wear it?

"Ginny!" Mom calls from the kitchen. "Hurry up. You don't want to be late."

"Coming!"

I pull a brush through my wispy hair, wishing for the millionth time that it was thick and wavy and dirty blond like Allie's. Instead, mine is the color of pine cones (the official state flower of Maine) and too thin to stay neatly in a ponytail.

Downstairs, I find Mom at the kitchen counter drinking coffee and fixing breakfast. She hands me a buttered plain bagel and studies my outfit.

"I would rethink the pith helmet," she says.

"Dad gave it to me for Christmas, and I've been dying to wear it somewhere," I tell her.

"I know, but it's a pretty unusual hat."

A pith helmet, also called a safari hat, is a lightweight cloth-covered helmet that protects your head from both sun and rain. I don't want to take it off. The weight of it is like Dad's hand on my head saying, *I'm here with you, Ginny.*

"Dad would let me wear it," I argue.

I can tell Mom doesn't agree. She sucks in her lips and inhales deeply. Then she plucks the hat off my head and puts it on top of the microwave.

"Skip the hat for today," she says. "See what the camp and the other kids are like, and then if you want to wear it tomorrow, you can."

This time I don't argue. I watch Mom as she zips feverishly around the kitchen. She unloads the dishwasher, pours herself an extra-large traveler mug of coffee, writes a note for Allie that she's taking me to camp, grabs her keys, and is standing at the door to the garage, all before I've halfway finished my bagel.

"Time to go, Ginny. You can finish breakfast on the way."

As Mom goes into the garage to start the car, I grab the pith helmet from the top of the microwave and shove it into my backpack with my lunch.

It's my hat, and I'm going to wear it.

<hr />

Mom and I find the registration table and stand in the H–P line. This place has a bunch of different camps, so there are tons of kids waiting.

When it's my turn, I step forward and say, "Ginny Pierce, reporting for geography camp." As a joke, I give her an official military salute.

She doesn't even crack a smile.

Instead, she adjusts her green visor and scans her clipboard for my name. She makes a check mark, then starts flipping through a stack of laminated name tags until she finds mine.

"Here you go," she says, handing it to me. "As you know, we didn't have enough kids signed up for the geography camp, so it was canceled. But you can choose from any of the other camps we offer since you're already paid up."

My jaw drops. I would say it falls to somewhere near Antarctica, which is at the very bottom of the world.

"Geography camp is *canceled*?"

"You didn't get the letter?" the woman asks.

"*Canceled?*" I repeat in a much higher voice.

Mom puts her hand on my shoulder so I don't screech again. She asks the woman, "What letter?"

"We sent out a letter asking campers to select a new option two weeks ago. You had the choice then to get a refund or choose a new program."

Two weeks ago we were in the middle of saying goodbye to Dad, packing up our house, and moving here. So the camp letter was either sent to our old house or got missed in all the commotion.

I wait for Mom to get angry, to tell this woman how much I've been looking forward to this camp..

But she doesn't. She just presses her lips together in a straight line and makes a noise like *hmphh*. Then she picks up a camp brochure lying on the table and holds it so we can both read it.

"What else looks fun, Ginny?" she asks, her voice steady as a drumbeat. This is Rational Mom. She's almost as frustrating as Military Mom sometimes. "They have jewelry making, ceramics, LEGO engineering, drawing, robotics, Irish dance, photography. Oh, and weaving. Weaving what? Cloth? Baskets? Pot holders?"

"No, thank you," I say. My voice is still abnormally high. I clear my throat.

The woman frowns at me, disappointed. "You don't want to try another camp, princess?"

I am not a princess—I'm going to be a famous *geographer*. I can recite all fifty states in reverse alphabetical order. Wyoming is first. Then Wisconsin. Then West Virginia.

I say, "Thank you, but I don't want to weave baskets. I want to learn how to calculate time from latitude and longitude."

There's a pricking at the back of my eyes, but I can't start crying about a camp being canceled. Even if that's what I feel like doing.

Mom excuses us and pulls me aside. She leans down and says, "I know you're upset. And I know you don't want to do a different camp, but we're already here, so why not try something else? If you don't like it, you don't have to come back."

Mom's always saying that when you're a military family, you don't dwell on things you can't change. You just pick up your beans and keep rolling.

I reach into my pocket and rub my new compass with my thumb. I think about how maybe when Dad gets back we can go geocaching together somewhere. I tell myself this isn't my only opportunity.

After a few deep breaths, I head back to the table and tell the lady, "I'll try photography, please."

Mom gives my shoulder a squeeze, which means *Good job, Ginny.* I'm picking up my beans, which makes her happy.

The lady makes a *tsk, tsk* noise as she checks a paper on her clipboard. "I'm sorry, princess. Photography is full."

"I am not a princess," I say, speaking slowly and emphatically. I scan the brochure. "How about pottery?"

I picture myself learning to use one of those pottery wheels that spins the clay while you shape it. It's not the same as discussing how Mount Kilimanjaro has *three* volcanic cones, but it might be interesting. I could even make a vase in the shape of a volcano and put red flowers in it to mimic an eruption.

The lady checks again. "Full, I'm afraid. The camps here are very popular."

Did they forget to advertise their geography program? The hill Taumatawhakatangihangakoauauotamateaturipukakapikimaungahoronukupokaiwhenuakitanatahu in New Zealand got a new sign in 2007, which has helped make it a great photo opportunity and tourist attraction for geography and word nerds.

"But," the lady adds, "there *is* a slot available in jewelry making! It's a three-week program. How about that?"

"Great!" Mom chirps. "She'll take it."

I don't answer. I can't. I'm practically frozen with disappointment. I'm a gigantic disappointment glacier.

I came here to meet other geography lovers and do cartography. Instead, I'm going to be making jewelry. For *three weeks*. I don't wear jewelry—I don't even like jewelry.

It's totally, completely, and stupidly unfair. Like everything else that's happened lately.

"All righty, then!" the green visor lady says, sounding triumphant. "You'll be in the main building, room 213. Head over there and get settled, princess."

This time I don't bother to correct her.

I look at Mom. If Dad were here, he'd be ready with a pep talk, something about silver linings or how the best things come from the biggest mistakes. He'd probably have a new fact for me that he'd been saving up. Something epic to take my mind off how horrible this is.

But Mom just says, "Chin up—it's not so bad."

That's it? *It's not so bad?*

"Sure, Mom," I reply. "And the San Andreas Fault line isn't so bad either."

"Huh? What's that?" asks the lady.

"It's an eight-hundred-mile-long crack in California where two tectonic plates rub against each other as they move in different directions," I tell her. "It's ten miles deep, and scientists believe it's headed for a major earthquake. One day Los Angeles and San Francisco could be side by side."

The lady stares back at me, her lips pursed. "Are you all right, princess?"

"She's fine—thank you for your help," Mom says, clipping my name tag to my shirt and steering me out of the line.

I follow her, feeling like my life now resembles California—carved into pieces by a giant fault line.

Fact: In the United States, there are two towns named Santa Claus. They can be found in Indiana and Georgia.

Mom leads me to the main building. I move slowly, still reeling from the fact that my dream camp was canceled.

Considering I've just left a school I really liked, moved to another state, and said goodbye to my dad for six months, you'd think something like a camp program not working out would be a drop in the bucket. But it isn't. Geography camp was helping me hold it together. It was *my* glue.

Mom goes into peppy-coach mode. "Don't let anyone know you're disappointed about being in jewelry camp. A good attitude goes a long way."

"I'd much rather talk about my *altitude* than my attitude," I reply.

I hope Mom will laugh, but she just clamps her lips together again and looks concerned. "Sometimes you have to give things a chance, Ginny. It wouldn't hurt you to have a few other interests."

Is that what Mom thinks I'll be doing here at camp—picking up a new hobby?

I remember the time she signed me up for gymnastics when I was five just because Allie was taking it, and they had another class at the same time for my age group. I brought a book and sat in the corner and read. They couldn't even get me to do a forward roll down the wedge.

Afterward, Mom told Dad how I wouldn't even try and just sat out and missed all the fun.

I know she wishes I were more like Allie sometimes. An easier kid who was into more normal things.

She fiddles with her car keys. She seems torn on whether to leave me here. "Have fun?" she says, like a question.

"I'll try."

I can tell Mom is considering giving me a hug, but there are kids streaming by. So she waves awkwardly and says, "Pick you up at three o'clock."

I wave back and watch her disappear around the corner. I wait ten more seconds, then pull my pith helmet from my backpack and clap it on my head. Now I have Dad with me at least.

I go inside the building and follow the signs to room 213. It's laid out like an ordinary classroom with desks lined up in rows. Jewelry kits are already set out at each place.

I take a seat, reminding myself to smile at the girls sitting around me. Unfortunately, no one smiles back. Instead, they stare.

"What's that on your head?" one girl asks.

"It's a safari hat," I tell her. "But it's not just for safaris—you can use it for sun, rain, whatever. Even US Marines wear them in some places."

I take it off and offer it to her to examine.

She shakes her head *no* and looks away. The other girls look away also. Apparently Mom was right about the hat.

I quickly stow it in my backpack and examine the kit in front of me. It has a bunch of different strings and beads, a sewing needle, and a paper printout of a very complicated pattern.

The instructor introduces herself as "Manda, like *panda*."

I love giant pandas. They have no natural predators in the wild, due to their size, strength, and isolated habitat. Plus, they're incredibly cute. As I'm thinking about pandas, everyone else picks up their supplies and begins stringing beads. Their fingers move so fast it looks like they're doing sign language.

How do they know what to do already?

Manda keeps talking, but I'm so busy watching everyone's hands that I don't listen carefully. Then I hear her say something about Russia and one of its former capitals, Saint Petersburg.

I perk up, relieved to have a way to join in the discussion.

"Are you Russian?" I ask Manda. "Or is your family Russian? Did you know that all astronauts going to the International Space Station must learn Russian?"

Manda frowns at me. "Huh? Why do you think I'm Russian?"

I look sideways at the girl next to me, as if to say, *Isn't it obvious?* The girl shakes her head *no*, as if it isn't.

Adam and Shuri would have understood. They would probably have asked the same question.

"Because you were talking about one of its most famous cities, Saint Petersburg, and you said *Russia* a bunch of times," I remind her politely.

"Yeah, because those are the names of the beading patterns we're using today—the Russian spiral, the double Saint Petersburg chain, and the Russian chevron chain," Manda replies. "Do you need...help?"

She says *help* like I'm the opposite of smart. I feel my ears get hot.

"No, I'm fine, thanks," I mumble.

I pick up my thread and start jamming beads onto it, not even bothering to follow one of the patterns in front of me, which all look more like sewing than beading. The patterns do sound intriguing, though, and must have their roots in Russian jewelry making or they wouldn't have those names.

I slide beads onto thread for what feels like ten hours. It's probably thirty minutes. Everyone is working diligently, and no one is talking about anything interesting. I recite all the world capitals alphabetically in my head, but the entire list takes me less than three minutes.

My brain is so bored.

I grab a pencil and doodle the shape of Iceland (capital: Reykjavík) onto my pattern paper. Iceland is fascinating. Eleven percent of it is covered in glaciers, and it was one of the last places on earth to be inhabited by humans.

I know I'm probably the only person here who cares about Iceland, but after another few excruciating minutes of quiet beading, I can't help myself. I have to talk about something.

I search the file cabinet in my brain for one of my most fun facts.

"*Psst*," I whisper to the girl on the other side of me, not the one who asked about my hat.

This girl looks over, her expression friendly. "Do you need help?" she asks, gesturing at my project.

Why does everyone here think I need help? We're making bracelets, not building suspension bridges.

"No, thank you. I was just wondering if you knew that everyone in Vietnam celebrates their birthday on New Year's Day? In Vietnam, and in Korea too, people traditionally measure their age by the number of lunar years they have lived in. So they're automatically one year old when they're born."

In a heartbeat, the girl's expression changes from friendly to freaked out.

I feel myself shrink, and I turn away so the girl can't see my face. My right temple starts throbbing, then my right eyelid.

I raise my hand.

"What's up?" asks Manda, absorbed by her phone. "Do you need more beads?"

"No," I say. "I have a headache. Can I go outside for a minute?"

Manda bites her lip and looks worried. She types something into her phone, and a second later I hear it *ding* as she receives a message. Then she says, "Um, I guess so. Take someone with you, okay?"

"Thanks, but I'm fine going alone." I pick up my backpack, relieved I brought my fact box with me. I really need it right now.

Manda looks up at last, her eyebrows pulled tight together again. "You're not supposed to. Can you go with her?" she says, eyeballing a girl a few rows ahead of me.

The girl has a long side braid of glossy black hair and an armful of friendship bracelets, the kind that are made with shiny embroidery floss knotted into different patterns. She looks like she's Allie's age, or maybe older.

65

Braid girl places her bracelet down on her desk. She carefully lays out the beads she was planning to use next and knots her thread, so the other beads won't slip off while she's gone. Then she stands up and walks out of the room. I follow.

Out in the hallway, I say, "I'm sorry you had to stop working to come out with me."

"It's okay," she says.

I hear Dad in my head. *Most people are nice if you just give them a chance. Be friendly.*

"I'm Ginny. I just moved here."

"Yeah, from North Carolina, right?" the girl says, flipping her braid back over her shoulder. It's so long that it hangs almost to her waist.

I look at her, amazed. "How'd you know that?"

"Because you just moved in across the street from me. Your sister has been at my house a bunch of times. You guys don't look anything alike, by the way."

"Yeah, I know." To change the subject, I ask, "What's your name?"

"Supriya. My younger brother is Rihan."

"Oh, right." Allie has been talking about a kid named Rihan who's obsessed with zombies. I met him for two seconds the other day when he knocked on our door looking for her.

He asked me if I believe in the undead. I don't. But Allie and Mom love to stay up late watching zombie horror movies together and scream when people get eaten. If I try to watch one, all I can think about is how illogical it is to be scared of zombies. They're incredibly slow and easy to run away from.

"The exit's this way," Supriya says, leading me through the halls.

We pass rooms filled with kids doing all kinds of crafty things. I can't help but wonder which classroom would have been my geography camp.

My shoulders slump. I miss Adam and Shuri. I miss my dad. I miss talking to people who like the same things I like.

"What's wrong?" Supriya asks, pushing open the door to the outside. "Are you sick?"

"No."

Supriya continues to watch me, clearly wanting an explanation for why she isn't at her desk beading right now. I need to either throw up or say something.

"I just needed a break," I say finally, sitting down on

a bench. With all the campers inside, it's quiet. Peaceful. Maybe I could just wait out here until three o'clock.

Supriya sits down beside me and plays with the knotted end of one of her bracelets.

I study her. "Is your family originally from India?"

"Yeah," she says warily. "Why?"

"There was a girl, Giti, at my old school, and her family is from India—"

"We don't all know each other, if that's what you're about to ask me." She crosses her arms and glares at me.

"Of course you don't! There are over a billion people in India. Anyway, that's not what I was going to say—I just think India's really interesting. Giti's family is originally from Delhi, and—"

She holds up her hand. "Can we talk about something else?"

"Oh, sure. Sorry." I was going to mention how impressive it is that India has twenty-three official languages. The United States doesn't even have one! Instead, I open my backpack and pull out my fact box.

"What's your favorite place?" I ask her. "I'll tell you a cool fact about it. It can be in the US if you want."

Supriya looks doubtful, but says, "Okay. Ummm, New York City?"

"Perfect." I flip through my box until I find the right card. "Did you know that every year, New York City moves approximately one inch farther away from London?"

"No way," says Supriya. "How do you even know that?"

"Because scientists measure it. The earth's surface is made up of tectonic plates, which are pieces that fit together like a jigsaw puzzle. And they're very slowly moving all the time. In fact, they move at about the same rate as your fingernails grow—one to two inches per year."

I explain about tectonic plates and continental drift and how the map of the world used to look very different.

Supriya looks slightly amazed when I'm done, as if I've just told her that dinosaurs aren't extinct and there's a real, live brachiosaur at the National Zoo.

"It's true," I insist. "I've been studying it."

"You mean, for a test or something?"

"No—just because I like it."

She looks at me curiously. "So what are you doing in jewelry-making camp?"

"I'm not. I mean, I *am*, but I was supposed to be in the geography camp here, only they canceled it. So now

I'm making a bracelet I'll never wear because I'm pretty bad at beading."

Supriya holds up her arm with its sleeve of bracelets. "I could teach you how to make these, if you want. And they won't have us bead all day—they'll teach us some really complicated stringing patterns later."

The thought of going back in that classroom for more silent bracelet-making makes my head hurt. Supriya eyes me, waiting for a response.

"Um, thanks, but I think I'd rather stay out here."

Supriya looks disappointed. She shrugs and plays some more with her bracelets.

I flip through the cards in my fact box, reading over my favorites. A minute goes by. Then another, and another.

Finally, Supriya says, "Sorry I snapped at you earlier. I get asked if I'm Indian a lot, and it's annoying. I didn't realize you were just interested in talking about India."

"I'm sorry too," I say. "I didn't mean to be annoying. I just find other countries and cultures fascinating."

I close up my file box and return it to my backpack. Maybe I can sit quietly in the corner of the classroom and read through my facts for the rest of the day.

"I can't believe you dragged that box here," Supriya says.

"I love facts. They never change. They're comforting."

Supriya rolls her eyes, but she's smiling.

"We should go back in, or Manda will come looking for us," she says. "Hang in there—we're going to learn a bunch of other stuff. You might even like it."

I seriously doubt that, but I nod anyway.

"It's too bad you can't just run your own geography camp," Supriya goes on. "Seems like you know enough about it. All you'd need are campers."

The idea is so obvious it practically flashes in front of me like a neon sign. My own geography camp!

If that isn't following my true north, what is?

Fact: The Taylor Glacier, in Antarctica, is considered one of the scariest-looking natural geographic features. It's famous for its Blood Falls, a five-story bloodred waterfall, which gets its color from the oxidized iron in the water and never freezes because of its high salinity.

I hop impatiently from one foot to the other as I wait in the carpool line at the end of the day. When Mom pulls up, I open the door before the car has even stopped moving.

Mom slams on her brakes, and the car bounces. "Careful, Ginny! The last thing we need right now is an accident, especially with Dad not here."

She says it casually, like he's at work and he'll be back in a few hours. Not like he's halfway around the world and we won't see him or hug him for half a year. How does she do that?

Allie studies the bumpy string creation I'm holding, which I pretended to work on this afternoon while I was planning my geography camp.

"Nice bracelet," she jokes.

I ignore her. "Has Dad called? I really need to talk to him."

"No, he hasn't," Mom replies. She hums as she steers us out of the parking lot. "Tell us about jewelry camp. Did you have fun?"

"No. It was terrible."

The humming stops. "C'mon, Ginny. It couldn't have been terrible—it's *camp*. I want you to think of two good things that happened to you today."

"Fine." I rack my brain. "Number one, we ate lunch outside, and it wasn't too buggy. And number two, I came up with a really good idea."

"Oh yeah?" Mom says. "What's that?"

"Since the awesome geography camp I was *supposed* to attend was canceled, I've decided I'm going to run my own."

Silence. Like beading silence, only more silent.

"You can't do that," Allie says.

"Sure I can," I tell her. What's the point of all of my reading and fact-collecting if I'm not going to share it with anyone? I don't have to wait to be an adult to have an impact as a geographer. I can get other kids interested in it now.

Besides, I love a project. Dad and I always have a project to work on—like when we made the bird feeder and the homemade telescope.

"No, Ginny," Allie sputters. "I don't mean you won't be *able* to do it. I mean you *shouldn't* do it."

"Why not?"

She smacks her forehead. "A million reasons. Seriously! Mom, can you tell her, please?"

Mom glances back at me in the rearview mirror. She looks skeptical. "How will you find campers?" she asks. "And how will you run it?"

I'm glad she asked, because I thought about that all afternoon.

"I'm going to email the principals at the local elementary and middle schools and ask them to send out a note to their school's email list," I explain. "I'll also post a flyer at the library, and one at the big grocery store. They have flyers for guitar lessons and French conversation groups, so why not a geography camp?"

"Hmm. I don't know about tha—" Mom begins.

Allie cuts her off. "Mom, you *cannot* let Ginny email the principal of my new school and spam everyone with her dumb idea. *Please.*"

"It's not dumb," I inform her. "Most Americans don't know where Zambia is located. *That's* dumb."

"I don't know where Zambia is, and I'm just fine," Allie mutters.

"Where are you planning to hold this camp?" Mom asks, ignoring my sister.

"Our house, obviously."

Mom shakes her head. "I'm sorry, Ginny, but we don't have enough space in this house for a camp."

"She'd only need space if kids actually wanted to come," Allie points out. "Which they won't."

"My jewelry camp has twenty kids, Allie. And geography is significantly more interesting than beading. Therefore, I bet I can get at least ten."

Allie groans but doesn't respond.

After a minute of no one speaking, Mom says, "Let me think on it for a bit, okay? Tell me more about the camp today. With details, please."

"I already told you—it was terrible. I had trouble following the patterns they were doing; I wore my pith helmet even though you told me not to; I asked the teacher if she was Russian but she isn't; and no one wanted to hear about how everyone in Vietnam has the same birthday."

"Ginny!" Allie shrieks. "Grow *up*. It was fine to be a supernerd in elementary school and talk about which mountains are the tallest or whatever, but now you're going into middle school. When you meet people, ask them if they play soccer. If they have a dog. If they like *pizza*."

Allie's told me this before. Several times. But I never do it because I don't care whether other people have pets or like soccer and pizza.

"Allie, I can't *help* liking the things that I like. I can't change my fundamentals. Can anyone? Can *you* stop liking basketball?"

"Who even uses the word *fundamentals*?" Allie huffs. "Just talk normally."

"Allie, stay out of this, please," Mom says, trying to smooth over the situation. "I'm sure tomorrow will go better, Ginny. Sometimes it takes a day to get used to new things. And I have to agree with Allie here—it wouldn't hurt to ask a few kids what their summer plans are or what school they go to."

I pause to ponder this. It's clear Mom is not on my side about my brilliant camp idea yet. It would be better to spend the afternoon strategizing before I tell her the rest of my plan because I'm pretty sure she won't like it. But it also might be wise to float the idea now, so I can nag her about it all evening if she says no.

"Mom?" My foot jiggles, making the car's floor mat clatter. "I'd like to get started creating my own camp right away. So can I just skip jewelry camp? Like, skip the whole thing?"

Mom sighs. "Really? You don't even want to give it one more try?"

"Please?" I say, a note of panic in my voice. "Dad wouldn't make me go."

"That's not fair, Ginny. Dad's not here." Mom honks her horn at the car in front of us, still sitting at the green light. It moves, and we make a right-hand turn.

A minute of silence ticks by. Then another. I wonder if I need to beg some more.

At last, she says, "I suppose if you're dead set against it, then you don't have to go back."

I feel a rush of relief. "Thank you, Mom!"

I can't wait to call Dad and tell him about my plan. He'll love the idea of me running my own camp. It's just the sort of thing he would tell me to do if he were here.

I picture it—kids seated at picnic tables in our backyard. I've attached a huge whiteboard and a map to the twin maple trees back there, and I'm holding a long stick, explaining why South America looks like it could tuck right into Africa if you pushed them together. (Tectonic plates again—they used to be attached!)

Allie pokes me in the knee and interrupts my daydream.

"What?" I say, poking her back in the shoulder.

"Ginny, listen," she says. "Nobody wants to go to camp to learn geography. It'd be like having a camp for kids to practice long division."

"Long division is basic math," I tell her. "It's completely different. I'm talking about a camp discussing the land, features, and phenomena of Earth."

Allie shakes her head as if I'm hopeless. "Fine. It's your funeral." She leans forward between the front seats. "Mom, can we stop and get a pizza? I'm starving, and I'm playing basketball later."

"Pizza sounds good to me," Mom replies.

Basketball, pizza, and more basketball. That's what I live with. No wonder I dream about running off to Reykjavík.

Fact: Australia is wider than the moon.
Also, if the earth were a nickel, the moon
would be a coffee bean.

When I open my eyes the next morning, there's a moment
before my brain is fully awake, and I think I'm in my old
room in Fayetteville.

I feel sleepy and content.

Then my vision comes into focus and I see the crack
in the ceiling and the double window next to my bed. I
realize I'm in Silver Spring and there are only three people in this house instead of four.

I have to be the glue, I remind myself. So I get up and
pull on yesterday's cargo shorts.

Once I'm dressed, I head downstairs. I want to video
chat with Dad about my camp idea. I tried calling him
last night, but there was no answer, so I sent him an
email describing my plan and asking for advice.

In the kitchen, I find Mom hunched over the counter, staring at her phone.

"Morning, Mom."

"Mmmmph," she replies.

"Have you heard from Dad?" I ask hopefully.

Mom shakes her head. Then she makes a weird noise, like a mix between a gasp and a shriek. She speed-walks past me and yells up the stairs, "Allie! Wake up! Come down, quick."

Panicked, I ask, "What's going on? Is it Dad? Is he okay?"

She looks at me. "Good—you're dressed. I can drop you off first, and then zip back here to get Allie and drop *her* off, then pick up a coffee, then be back by, hmmm, nine-ish?"

What is she talking about? Drop Allie off where? "Mom, *is Dad okay?*"

She blinks hard and nods. "Yes, of course. I mean, I think so."

My knees feel wobbly. I thought for sure she'd just gotten bad news about Dad.

"Then what are you talking about?" I ask. "Drop me off where? I'm not going to camp today. You said I didn't have to."

Mom's face and ears turn tomato red. "Ginny, listen. I just got offered a great catalog project, and it pays really well, and it could lead to a lot more work. But the turnaround time is fast. The original writer they hired canceled, and they can't change the date at the printer—"

"So you've got a lot of work to do," I cut in.

"Yes."

"No problem. I'll stay out of your way."

Mom does freelance copywriting for brochures and ads and catalogs, which means she does work for lots of different companies and can do it from anywhere. She likes it because it's usually hard for military spouses to find work since they're always moving. The problem is, she never knows when she's going to have projects and when she isn't. Normally we're in school so it doesn't matter, but now it's July.

Mom zooms into action, making breakfast. She whips out my Asia place mat from a set of plasticized maps I bought with my own money when I was eight—I call them my *place-maps*—and puts it down on the table, plopping a buttered bagel on top for me.

"Just staying out of the way is not going to do it," she says.

I don't like the sound of that. "What do you mean?"

Mom looks down at the other bagel she's slicing. "I'm calling the local community center and signing your sister up for camp there, and you're going back to jewelry camp."

"*No!* You said I didn't have to go back."

Allie shuffles into the kitchen, still in her pajamas, and grabs a freshly toasted bagel for herself. "Why did you wake me up?" she grumbles. "And why is Ginny yelling?"

Mom explains the situation, glancing at the clock every few seconds like it's a ticking bomb.

"No way," Allie says. "I'm *not* going to some boring community center camp where they'll make us play freeze tag in the hallway. Besides, I'm supposed to video chat with Mara later."

"And *I'm* not going to jewelry camp," I chime in.

For once, Allie and I are in complete agreement about something.

Mom noisily refills her coffee mug, smacking the pot against the machine. "Well, I can't have you two running in and out of the house interrupting me all day."

Mom is looking very close to panicked right now. Even though she won't say it, because she and Dad told us that everything would be *just fine* while he's deployed, everything *is* noticeably harder now that he's not here. She and Dad have a long-standing argument about whether or not we should live on base because there's more support for military families there, and hardly any in civilian communities. But Dad prefers to live off base because there are more housing and school options. With this move, it wasn't even an option, because there's no family housing on base for Walter Reed.

I stare at my Asia place-map. My eyes land on Afghanistan, which is in the middle-left part of Asia, and I quickly slide my plate to cover it. I don't want to look at Afghanistan right now.

"At least let me go to a sports camp," Allie argues.

"We can't afford it—we've already paid for you to go to basketball camp in a few weeks. And I can't have any distractions. I need *quiet*."

"What if Ginny and I stay outside all day?" she offers. "We won't even come inside the house."

Mom looks skeptical. "That will never happen. You'll be in and out, doors slamming, banging around the kitchen, et cetera. I need this job to go well so I can get more work from this client. This is important for *all* of us."

"*No.*" Allie slams her hand on the counter. "I'm not going."

"*Allie*," Mom says warningly.

I don't blame Allie for not wanting to go to the community center. *I* don't want to spend another day beading when I could be planning a discussion with my future campers about the Pygmy tribes of the Congo. But Mom and Allie almost never fight, so watching them gives me a pit in my stomach. Is this what it's going be like without Dad around?

"Wait!" Allie says, looking over at me triumphantly. "I have an idea."

"Let's hear it," Mom says.

"Ginny can run her geography camp, and I'll help her with it."

"No, thanks," I reply. "You told me it was a terrible idea, remember? You said no one would want to come. Why would I want your help?"

"Because you don't want to go back to jewelry camp," she reminds me, her eyes shooting daggers.

Mom shakes her head and says, "Forget it—I'll spend the entire day playing referee between you two. Ginny, go brush your teeth and meet me in the car. You have seven minutes."

Mom looks at the clock again. I can almost hear her calculating how many minutes until we're gone and she can get to work.

"We won't fight," Allie pleads. "I promise. You know I'm too old for day camp. Dad wouldn't send me."

"Don't guilt me," Mom snaps. She's gripping her phone in one hand and her coffee mug in the other, and she looks mega stressed. Her hair is sticking up funny on one side. Dad calls it her duck fluff.

"If you let me stay home, I'll help Ginny with her camp and we won't fight," she promises.

Mom seems to consider the idea for another minute. "I don't know," she says with a sigh. "I hate making decisions like this without your dad."

Finally, she relents. "Okay, we'll try it today and see how it goes. I'm going up to my room now to work. If you need me, come and knock. But only if it's something serious."

"Got it," says Allie.

I don't say anything. I am not happy.

Allie's going to help me with my camp? How? She doesn't know where Uruguay is. I doubt she could find North Carolina on a map and we lived there for two years.

As soon as Mom is gone, I study Allie. She's wearing her favorite oversized pajama bottoms and neon tie-dye T-shirt. Her thick, wavy hair is pulled up in a messy bun, and she has a stack of rope bracelets on one wrist.

Allie was born cool. I know it, and she knows it, and everyone who meets her knows it. When we were younger, we played together. Stuffed animals, dolls, make believe. We used to play board games too, but once I started beating her, that stopped.

I don't know if things will ever go back to how they were when we were little. Dad says they will, and that sisters are sisters for life. But we are two very different people.

"I don't need your help with my camp," I tell her. "But thanks anyway."

Allie takes a large bite of her bagel and answers with her mouth full. "Good, because I'm not really going to help you. I was just trying to convince Mom to let us both stay home. And it worked. You're welcome."

I nod, as if I knew that was her plan all along. But as I leave the kitchen and head up to my room, I can't help feeling disappointed. For a minute I thought Allie really did want to help me. I thought maybe it would be the two of us working together on a shared project, the way Dad and I do.

It was a nice thought.

———————

Up in my room, I sit down at my desk to start thinking about my camp. But the conversation with Allie has zapped some of my enthusiasm. I page through my geography books and my pile of maps, hoping I'll find something inspiring.

I need to talk to Dad. He'll know what to do.

I find our tablet and call him. It rings and rings. When his voice mail beeps, I freeze for a second, unsure of what to say. I'm not used to leaving messages for him.

"Hi, Dad, it's Ginny. Um, I have an important question for you, and I need you to call me back. Oh, and how are you? What does Afghanistan look like? I love you. Um, okay, bye!"

It's nine o'clock in the morning here, so it's 5:30 PM there. I hope he'll call me back soon. I wonder if he's eating dinner. Who is he sitting with? What are they talking about? Is he wearing fatigues or his Sunday pants?

I decide to temporarily postpone camp planning and do some research on what Dad's doing. I find a bunch of YouTube videos of soldiers giving tours of military bases in different parts of the world. I know that for this post, Dad is working in a combat support hospital (or CSH, but pronounced *cash*). Working in a CSH seems like a safer deployment than his last one, where he was stationed with an infantry unit on an FOB, a forward operating base, because the CSH is farther from the action. Most patients are driven or helicoptered there from an FOB.

Dad told me that when soldiers are deployed, they're pretty much "on duty" all the time. They can sometimes work twenty-four hours a day, seven days a week. So most likely, Dad isn't sitting around enjoying dinner or

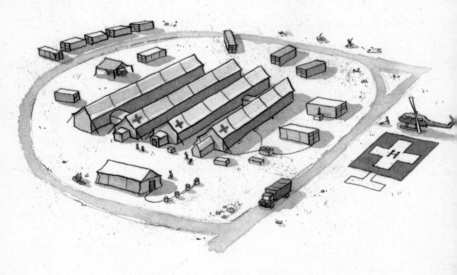

taking a walk and looking at the stars like he would on an evening at home. He's just working.

I watch a few more videos, wishing Dad would send us one of himself in his temporary home. Maybe this would be easier if I could actually *see* where he is. Then I start clicking on the headlines beneath some of the videos. Most of them are about attacks on US troops abroad.

TWO KILLED, THREE INJURED

FOUR DEAD IN A ROADSIDE BOMBING

HOSTILE INCIDENT RESULTS IN CIVILIAN CASUALTY

I pause on the word *casualty*. How can the word *casual* be part of a word that means the death or injury of someone in war? What's casual about that?

I sit at my desk, scrolling down the page and reading scary headline after scary headline. I read until the tablet's low battery message appears, warning me it's below 5 percent.

I turn it off and crawl onto my bed. I wrap myself tightly in my blanket and curl up on my side like the letter *C*.

C for *casualty*. Casualty. Casualty.

I hear Allie outside shouting and playing some game in the cul-de-sac with a few other kids. I hear Mom talking on the phone, then going up and down the stairs as she refills her coffee. I hear the mail carrier knock as he drops off a package.

The day crawls by. I stay in my bedroom and work on my Afghanistan map. Reading about Dad's deployment has made it more real. He isn't just not here—he's *there*. And right now, he feels as far away as the moon.

***

In the late afternoon, there's a knock on my bedroom door. I've been rereading my favorite biography of Marie Tharp, who, even though she was plotting the ocean floor, wasn't allowed on the research boat to gather data because she was a woman. Her story is the perfect distraction, about as far from what's going on in Afghanistan as I can find on my bookshelf.

"Come in."

It's Mom, looking pale and harried. "I need to run to the store to get a few things. Why don't you come with me?"

"No, thanks."

"I'd like your company," Mom says. "Meet me downstairs in two minutes, please."

She leaves before I can argue.

When we're in the car, Mom says, "I got an email from Dad."

She says it unceremoniously, as if it's not the best thing that's happened since we moved here.

"You *did*? Why didn't you tell me? Can I read it?"

"Of course. My phone's in my purse."

I root around until I find the phone and pull up her emails.

Dad's message is at the top of her inbox: *Very busy! Nice team here. More soon. Love.*

No news, no details, no *How's Ginny?* Just a stupid little eight-word email?

"That's *it*?" I shriek. "That's all he wrote?"

Mom takes her phone from me and puts it in the center console. She turns left at the end of our street to head toward the shopping plaza. "I thought you'd be happy we heard from him."

"I am, but do you know what's going on over there? It's a mess! He needs to tell us if he's in a safe place. And what it's like. And he needs to reply to my email and voice mail."

Mom takes a slow, measured breath before answering. "Maybe he can't respond right now—being at the CSH is different from when he was at training. But I know he'll get back to you as soon as he can. You just have to be patient."

"That's easy for you to say. You don't miss him like I do." The words tumble out before I can stop myself.

Mom looks at me sharply, her foot tapping the brake by accident and causing us both to lurch forward. We drive in silence until we reach the parking lot of the grocery store. She wants to snap at me; I can feel it. I cross my arms and kick the wheel well under the dashboard, angry at myself for acting like a brat.

When we're parked, she turns to me, her voice cool, and says, "I miss him terribly, Ginny. But this is what we signed up for—and I know that if he could write more, he would."

I stare out the window at the people going in and out of the store. They're all going home soon to have dinner with their family. Their *entire* family. They don't have a parent deployed halfway around the world.

Which, by the way, I did *not* sign up for. Dad did, long before he and Mom had me and Allie.

"I know I'm not the one you usually come to when you need advice," Mom says. "But I can tell you from experience that the secret to getting through deployments is to *keep busy*. What did you do today? What happened with planning your camp?"

I shrug but don't answer. It seemed like such a good idea yesterday when Supriya mentioned it. But now it just feels too hard. If it can't be the camp I was supposed to attend, with geocaching and all the bells and whistles, why bother?

Mom gathers up her keys and phone and purse. "Your camp idea is the reason I let you stay home today. If you're not going to do it, then you're going back to jewelry camp. And not because I'm *mean*, but because I know it's the best thing for you. Do you think your dad would want you moping in your room all day? That would break his heart. Keep busy."

Mom climbs out of the car and starts walking briskly toward the store. I have to jump out and jog to catch up with her.

"Fine," I say as we walk through the automated door.

"Fine what?"

"Fine, I'll do the camp. I'll start tomorrow."

"Okay," she says, wrestling a cart from the long line of them jammed together inside the doorway. "And remember—don't let perfect be the enemy of good."

"What does that mean?" I ask her.

"It means that the idea of achieving perfection, of getting exactly what we want, can sometimes prevent us from enjoying something that's good enough."

I don't know if she's talking about my camp idea or about Dad being gone. Maybe both. I follow behind her as she starts tossing food in the cart. Apples, bagels, cream cheese, milk. When we get to the meat section, I grab a packet of Dad's favorite brand of bacon.

"You know I don't like cooking bacon," Mom says. "Grease gets everywhere. Let's wait until Dad comes back and can cook it for us."

"I want the bacon," I tell her. "*I'll* make it."

I toss it in the cart and keep walking, feeling like I've planted a tiny flag on the summit of Mount Everest.

Fact: Antarctica is the only land on our planet not owned by any country. It's also the largest desert in the world—some parts of it haven't had rain or snow in over two million years.

The next morning, I take a pad of paper, a pen, and some colored pencils and head outside to brainstorm. Creating my own camp feels like a daunting task. For it to work, I'm going to need a really good plan.

I walk down our driveway and sit on a huge rock near the bottom so I can see the entire court. All the houses have front porches and pointy roofs and are painted pale colors like yellow or gray. They're close together and have small yards, unlike our old house in Fayetteville, which was on an acre.

The rock I'm sitting on is really round, like a ball, so I decide to pretend it's a globe and that I'm an ancient glacier atop its North Pole: tall and frozen and majestic.

Astride my globe rock, I make myself a to-do list:

1. Decide on camp location!
2. Recruit campers!
3. Plan activities!
4. Start camp!

I read somewhere that using exclamation points can help you achieve your goals. So can smiling.

Decide on camp location! is first. Our backyard is full of mosquitoes, so the obvious answer is our front porch, which is big and comfortable, with a swing and several chairs. I could even tape maps to the side of the house. Best of all, it's not technically *in* our house, which Mom said was off-limits.

Next, I need to *Recruit campers!* My original plan was to email a few principals and post flyers around town to try to find actual geography enthusiasts. Allie hated that idea, and she may have had a point. Anyway, now that I need this camp to start right away, I really only have one option—to ask the kids in the neighborhood.

It's not ideal, but Mom said, *Don't let perfect be the enemy of good.* The neighborhood kids are good enough. I could make flyers and walk them around Curtis Court so I can invite each kid in person.

I start working on my flyers. It's not easy finding words that rhyme with *facts*, other than *attacks*, *Zach's*, and *wax*. After a few tries, I come up with this:

Enjoy FACTS and SNACKS
at Ginny's Geography Camp!
Today at 11:00 a.m.
Ginny's front porch—15 Curtis Court
It's fun! It's FREE!
(Be ready to discuss your favorite continent!)

I add snacks to my to-do list. Then I make several copies of the flyer, using my best handwriting and vibrant colors, and head out to deliver them.

There's no answer at the first two houses on the left, but I see little-kid toys in both yards, so I slide a flyer under each front door.

Next up is the biggest house on Curtis Court. A girl on the front porch is wearing a smock and painting at an easel, looking in the opposite direction from me. She's completely focused on her work, and I approach quietly so I don't disturb her. By the time I'm standing behind her, she still hasn't turned around, so I reach out and stick the flyer in front of her face.

"Bah!" She drops her paint tube in fright and accidentally steps on it, causing a bright yellow worm to squirt across the porch floor. "Nooooo," she moans. "My cadmium yellow! That was the last bit I had."

"Whoops," I say. "Sorry about that."

She bends over to retrieve the tube, using the hem of her smock to wipe up the mess. She doesn't answer me.

"I'm really sorry," I say again, angry at myself for sneaking up on her instead of just saying hello. I start babbling. "I'm Ginny, by the way. Well, my *real* name is Virginia, which is cool, right? Because it's a name *and* a place. But I go by Ginny."

The girl blinks at me, her dark eyes as big and round as chestnuts. A second goes by. Then another.

"I'm Kayla," she replies finally. She holds her art smock slightly away from her body as it dries, so the fresh yellow stain won't leak onto her clothes. For an artist, she's extremely tidy. From her black hair, which is divided into rows of tiny braids and pulled back into a low ponytail, to her smock, to her clean white sneakers, there's not a speck of paint on her.

After staring at her for a minute, I remember my flyer, which is still in my hand.

"I hope you can come," I say, shoving the flyer toward her once again. I notice a dirty pair of boy's sneakers by her front door and make an educated guess. "Do you have a brother? He can come too."

Still holding her smock with one hand, Kayla takes the flyer with the other and reads it. "You're running a camp about...*geography*?" she asks. "Why?"

"To share amazing facts about our beautiful earth, of course!" I throw my arms out wide, as if I'm hugging the whole world. One of my hands smacks the easel and makes it shake. Kayla looks alarmed again.

So awkward. I can just imagine what Allie would do if she were with me. Probably clap a hand over my mouth and drag me off the porch.

"Sorry," I say quickly, steadying her canvas. She's painting a tree in the yard opposite hers, mixing yellow and blue on her palette to make various shades of green.

"Did you know that ginkgoes are the oldest existing tree species in the world?" I say.

She looks perplexed. "Huh?"

I point to the tree she's painting. "That's a ginkgo tree. Its fan-shaped leaves are found in fossil records that go back 225 million years, which means they date back to dinosaur times. It's considered a living fossil."

Kayla's eyebrows raise. I can feel myself doing it—I'm on fact attack, as Allie calls it.

"Do you have any pets?" I blurt out, remembering her advice.

"Yeeeeeess," Kayla says slowly. She squints her eyes at me, as if thinking hard. "We have a cat—Fisher."

"Cool. I wish we had a pet. My mom says we can't have one because we move too often. So I'll see you and your brother at my camp later?"

"Um, well, I usually paint most of the day," Kayla says. She shakes her smock out to air-dry the paint spot. "Or our babysitter takes us to the pool. And my brother, Jerome, is away at Space Camp."

"I usually study every day, so I can learn new facts." I'm babbling again. "That's why this will be such a good camp. And that's why you should come."

Kayla frowns. She's starting to look annoyed. "I'll see how much I can get done, okay?" she says, putting my flyer on a table. She turns back to her canvas to let me know I'm dismissed.

That did not go well but I'm not giving up. There are nine other houses on our street, and Supriya's brother, Rihan, is in the court playing basketball with Allie.

"Hi," I say, approaching them cautiously. No one responds. Rihan has the ball and shoots. Allie catches the rebound. They don't even look my way.

"Did Allie tell you about my camp?" I ask Rihan, holding out my flyer. "It's for all the kids who live on the street. It starts today."

Allie peeks at the flyer over Rihan's shoulder and then looks away, bouncing the ball extra hard against the asphalt. Her cheeks are pink. From embarrassment? From the heat?

Rihan takes my carefully colored flyer, folds it unevenly, and shoves it into his pocket, like an old gum wrapper.

He doesn't say anything. He just looks from me to my sister as if wondering what will happen next.

I turn to Allie. "Mom said you had to help me with camp if you were going to skip the community center, remember? So Rihan might as well come too."

Allie closes her eyes and shoots the ball blind. It swishes neatly through the hoop, and as she retrieves it, she says, "Maybe, Ginny—okay?"

I frown. *Maybe* isn't good enough. I switch tactics. "Rihan, did you know that if you traveled at the speed of light, you could reach Pluto in just four hours?"

"Oh," he says, not sounding particularly interested.

"Later, Ginny." Allie's voice is quiet but firm. "You're interrupting our game."

"Finish your game," I say, barely keeping my voice steady. "I'll see you both on our porch at eleven o'clock."

I walk off toward the next house to continue delivering my flyers. It feels like so many bricks are being piled onto my shoulders right now—the move, the deployment, the canceled camp. Anyone can carry one brick around all day, but can you carry a whole bagful? Can you keep adding one more?

Hoping Allie and Rihan didn't notice my shaky voice, I yell back over my shoulder, "It's going to be *great*."

Maybe if I say it enough times, it'll come true. I walk with my head high, but inside me something is sagging, like a flag at half-mast.

Fact: By the early fourth century, the ancient Romans had built a road network of nearly fifty-three thousand miles, connecting their vast empire to the capital city of Rome. That's where the saying "All roads lead to Rome" comes from. Some of these roads are still standing today, nearly seventeen hundred years later.

After I finish delivering the flyers, I retreat inside.

I find the tablet and try calling Dad again. I need his advice. How can I make this camp idea work if no one wants to come? I hit the video call button and wait, studying my anxious face on the screen. It rings and rings and no one answers.

Where is he?

I run upstairs and knock on Mom's door. "What is it?" she calls, in her *I'm working* voice.

I open the door and poke my head in. "Have you heard from Dad? I just tried calling him again and didn't get an answer. I really need his help."

"No, I haven't. He'll call or email as soon as he can."

She sounds annoyed. Annoyed that I need Dad, or annoyed that I'm interrupting her work? If the situation were reversed, and Dad was the parent here while Mom was deployed, he wouldn't brush me off when I asked about her.

"Never mind," I mutter, pulling the door closed to leave.

"Wait, Ginny," Mom says. She closes her eyes and takes a deep breath. "I'm sorry—you caught me right in the middle of something. How is your camp planning going? Is Allie helping?"

If it were Dad asking, I'd tell him everything. But Mom will just force me to go to jewelry camp if I tell her the truth.

So I say, "Yeah, it's going fine. I have to set up for it now."

Dad would know I'm lying. But Mom smiles, relieved, and says, "Oh yeah? Terrific! Keep me posted."

I shut the door, hard, and head downstairs.

Why did I decide to do this camp? I don't even want to do it anymore, and I'm stuck, because Mom is expecting me to and I've handed out all those flyers.

If we were still in Fayetteville, I could have pulled this off. I could have invited some kids from my school, the ones who also loved science facts. Hopefully the kids at my new magnet school here will be the same. But until school starts, the only people I have to hang out with are Allie and the kids in this neighborhood.

I grab my compass from my room and slip it into my pocket for good luck. Then I go down to the basement to see what we have to create a camp space.

I find our old plastic art easel and lug it up to the front porch. I clip my place-map of North America to it and stick a wooden spoon nearby to use as a pointer. I jot down a list of basic questions about the topography of the United States to get everyone warmed up (*What's the highest mountain in the United States? How many great lakes are there?*) and stick them in the tray of the easel.

It's hard to know what to focus on. The kids on the street are all different ages, and some of them may not even know how to read a map. At school we always do practice sheets when we learn a new unit in science or math, so I decide a worksheet is a good place to start. I run up to my room to get the geography workbook Dad got me for my birthday and take it down to the basement where we have the family computer and printer. I make a bunch of copies of one of the first pages, which is a word scramble of the fifty states. I consider writing a quiz about the fifty states as well, such as which US state is the only one to have an active diamond mine—Arkansas!—but worry it would take me too long.

I scrounge up a handful of pencils and some gold star stickers from the basement desk and take everything back up to the porch. There's a small table between the wicker rockers that I'll use as my camp counselor desk.

In case there are some younger kids who get bored or need a craft, I put a clear plastic bin of beads and string that I got as a gift a long time ago on the windowsill. I haven't touched it since first grade, so someone might as well use them.

I survey the porch, pleased that it's starting to look like a camp now. I tape up one of my flyers to the porch post, like a welcome sign. As I do, I remember that I promised snacks with the facts.

Running a camp is a lot of work. Like building Rome was for the Romans, I would imagine.

I head back into the house. In the pantry, I look through every shelf and bin hoping to find something exciting, like cheese popcorn or Twizzlers. But instead we have bags of granola, my mom's fiber bars, packets of onion soup mix, a canister of those really big, hard pretzels, and five cans of diced tomatoes.

This is not good. I need to improvise.

I grab a bowl from the cabinet and pour in some granola and cereal. I look for chocolate chips or mini marshmallows, something to make this trail mix a little more exciting, but there's nothing. Mom stopped buying exciting food about a year ago and started buying really boring stuff: veggie burgers, chicken breasts, and salads. She says she wants to get her "shape" back, but I think she's a perfectly fine shape already.

I take the hard pretzels and my bowl of trail mix out to the porch along with some paper cups and a pitcher of water. I read somewhere that you can study for four hours with the energy from just one peanut, so this should be enough to keep everyone sharp.

Now that all my supplies are together, I feel more hopeful. What if it *does* work? What if kids come and have a good time?

Dad will be so proud of me.

At 10:58 AM, I sit down and wait for camp to begin.

At 11:05, I'm still alone. Allie and Rihan disappeared into someone's backyard while I was setting up, and I have no idea where they are or if they're coming.

At 11:10, I drink a glass of water and eat a few handfuls of granola. It's dry and sticks in my throat, so I have more water. Things don't look good.

Finally, at 11:12, a little kid from two doors down skips up the front walk. She says, "Hi, I'm Lucia. I got your flyer. Is this camp?"

She talks loudly, as if she's had a cold and her ears are clogged. Or maybe that's just how she talks. It doesn't matter either way because I'm happy to have even one real, authentic, enthusiastic camper.

"Hi, Lucia, I'm Ginny," I say. "How old are you?"

"Six," she says. Then, looking around at my empty porch, "Is anyone else coming?"

"I don't know," I reply. I pick up the snack bowl and hand it to her. "Here, have some trail mix."

Lucia sticks her hand in the bowl and swishes it around. She frowns. "It's just cereal! Where's the chocolate?"

I knew it needed chocolate. "This is healthy trail mix," I tell her. "It's better for you."

She looks doubtful. Luckily, a fact pops into my head that's perfect for the occasion. "Did you know that people in Switzerland eat more chocolate than anyone else in the world? About twenty-six pounds per person every year. That's like two hundred forty chocolate bars, *each*."

Lucia's eyes grow wide. "Really?"

"Yes. And Switzerland is a beautiful country. It's pretty small—about the size of Massachusetts and Connecticut combined—but it has around fifteen hundred lakes and ten thousand mountains."

As we're talking, I hear dribbling behind me. It's Allie, coming up the walk. I'm so grateful I want to hug her. She tosses her basketball into the wicker basket on the porch and then plops down on the swing.

"Hi," I say tentatively, unsure how she's going to act. "Lucia, this is my sister, Allie."

"Yeah, I know," she says. "She came to my—"

"Hi, Lucia," Allie cuts in swiftly.

I hope Allie doesn't keep interrupting everyone. I'm wondering if I should get started when I see Rihan coming out his front door and crossing the court toward us.

"I dodged three zombies to get here," Rihan says dramatically as he climbs our porch steps. "We should get a hunting party together."

"Yeah, we should do that later," I say. I'm thrilled to have an additional camper, even if it's a zombie hunter.

"Zombies?" says Lucia nervously.

"Not really," I whisper to her.

She nods but looks uncertain.

Across the circle, I see Kayla heading toward us as well.

"Hi, Kayla," I say as she sits down across from me. "Should we wait another minute to see if anyone else is coming?"

"Jack and Emily aren't home," Lucia says, pointing at the house next to ours, and then to other houses across the cul-de-sac in turn. "And Autumn's at horseback riding camp, Supriya's at jewelry camp, and Jerome's at Space Camp."

Hmm. This kid knows everything about everyone. I should have asked her to be my camper recruiter.

"Okay, then, let's start," I say. "My name's Ginny, and my sister and I just moved here a few weeks ago. I love geography and plan to be a geographer when I grow up."

"Is that really a thing?" asks Rihan.

I nod. "There are different kinds of geographers— cartographers, urban and regional planners, geoscientists. Stuff like that. I want to be a geoscientist. Anyway, we have seven continents to discuss, so let's get started."

"Seven condiments?" Lucia says.

"*Continents*," I say slowly. "You know, large land-masses like Antarctica and Australia."

I grab the wooden spoon and point to the map I clipped on the easel. I feel a buzz of excitement about finally getting to discuss my favorite subject. It's one of the things I've missed most about Dad being away. "Let's start with our home continent—North America. Does anyone know what *countries* make up North America?"

Lucia raises her hand and says, "North America!" Then she grins, like she's going to get a prize.

"Good guess," I tell her. "But not quite. Anyone else?"

I look at Rihan, who, according to Allie, is twelve but going into sixth grade like me. He must know at least one of the countries. He catches my eye, then looks down, muttering, "The United States."

"Yes!" I say. "What other countries or lands make up North America? And did you guys know that the longest river in the US is actually the Missouri, *not* the Mississippi? Everyone gets that wrong—even teachers."

Allie holds up her hands, palms facing me, and says, "Chill out, Ginny. We're not at school, remember?"

She's right. This isn't school, and I'm not a teacher. Unfortunately, I spent too much time thinking about whether I would be able to get any campers and not enough about what to do with them once I had them.

I have one chance to get this right. If I fail, it's over.

Fact: There can be as many as ten million viruses in a single drop of seawater. These viruses destroy up to half the bacteria in the oceans every day.

After another moment of awkward silence, I repeat my question about North America. I'm hoping someone will answer and give me enough time to think of a new plan.

This time, Kayla raises her hand. She makes sure everyone is listening, then says, "North America includes the US, all the countries of Central America, all the island nations of the Caribbean, Bermuda, Canada, and, um, oh yeah—Greenland."

My jaw drops. I would have bet a hundred dollars I was the only person here who knew that Greenland is on the North American tectonic plate and is therefore geographically part of North America. Most people assume it's linked to Europe because politically it's part of the

Kingdom of Denmark. Basically, Greenland doesn't fit in anywhere. It's one of my favorite sneaky facts about geography, which is why I have it written on a special pink index card in my fact box.

I stare at Kayla for a minute, surprised by her level of geographic knowledge.

"That's right," I reply finally. Kayla smiles, looking pleased with herself, and brushes some invisible dirt off her shorts. "How'd you know that?"

"I read it somewhere," she says.

"But *where* did you read it?"

She scrunches up her face, like she's thinking hard. "I don't remember."

She doesn't remember where she read it, but she remembers all the areas of North America, including Greenland? Does she have a selective photographic memory?

I would *love* a photographic memory. Then I could remember absolutely everything about everything. Other than having Dad back home, it's my greatest wish.

Everyone is staring at me, waiting to see what's next. Lucia points at the pile of papers beside me. "What are those?"

"Oh, right," I say, flustered. I reach for the word scrambles and begin handing them out. But when I get to Allie, she says, "We don't want to do homework. It's summer."

Rihan and Kayla don't look thrilled either. Only Lucia takes her paper happily, although she probably can't read well enough yet to do a word scramble.

I'm going to lose them. I managed to get four kids to my camp, and I truly don't know what to do with them. I wish I knew how to set up a geocaching treasure hunt. Maybe I could have everyone create a 3D map of the neighborhood?

I have to think fast. What can we talk about that everyone will enjoy? Allie loves sports stats. And team rankings. And all kinds of games.

That's it—trivia about the fifty states! Everyone likes trivia because it's kind of like a game.

I get up, turning the map of North America around so no one can read it, and clip on a fresh piece of paper. Then I face my group. Everyone is about to discover just how awesome geography can be.

"There are twenty-one states whose names end with the letter *A*," I announce. "Can anyone name them?"

I aim my wooden spoon pointer at Rihan. "Rihan, do you want to start? Can you name five?"

Rihan grimaces as if I'd said I had a highly contagious and deadly virus. So does Kayla. Allie's face turns red.

"Rihan," I try again, "how about you name *one* state that ends with the letter *A*?"

Rihan coughs and his eyes flit to Allie as if asking what to do. Allie pretends not to notice and studies the porch ceiling.

Finally, after an agonizing minute, Rihan mumbles, "Alabama."

"Great work!" I write it down on the paper. "Only twenty to go. Allie? Your turn."

She shakes her head. I'm not sure she knows any, honestly. She can remember the score of every Tar Heels basketball game last season, but school stuff doesn't seem to stick. This year her grades were more C's than B's.

I look at Lucia, who raises her hand and says, "We live in Maryland."

"Excellent," I tell her.

"It ends with a *D*," she adds.

"Very, very good." She is only six, after all.

No one else makes a guess, so I look at Allie again. "Can you name a state that might be near us here in

Maryland?" I'm tempted to mention that one of them is her sister's name, and one is the state we just moved from.

Allie rolls her eyes and looks bored.

"Oh, *I'll* do it," Kayla grumbles. "Alaska, Iowa, North Dakota, South Dakota, California, Georgia, Florida, Louisiana, Arizona, Indiana, Nevada, Montana, Minnesota, Nebraska, Pennsylvania, Virginia, North Carolina, South Carolina, West Virginia."

She counts them on her fingers, stopping to take a breath and think.

"Wow," says Lucia, looking at her in awe. "How'd you know so many states?"

"I'm going into seventh grade," Kayla replies. "And we have a huge world map in our kitchen."

Ha! So that's how she knew all the countries in North America.

"You guys have twenty states total now," I remind everyone, scribbling them all down. "We only need one more!"

"PHILADELPHIA!" shrieks Lucia. "That's where my grandma lives."

"Great guess because it ends in *A*, but it's a city, not a state," I tell her. "You can do it!"

To my delight, every one of them seems to be thinking hard.

"Huge pretzel to the person who can come up with the answer!" I say, pulling one out of the container and dangling it in the air.

"Those pretzels are stale, Ginny," Allie says. "I'm pretty sure Mom meant to throw those out when we moved."

"Does that mean you don't know the answer?" I ask her.

"I don't *want* to know the answer."

I don't believe her. Not for a second. Everyone wants to know the answer to a question no one else can guess. Everyone wants to feel smart, don't they?

Finally, Rihan blurts out, "Oklahoma!"

I burst into applause. "Yes! Nice job, Rihan."

He looks pleased with himself. He even stands up to take a bow.

"That was great work, everyone," I continue, adding a huge A-plus to the paper with the list of state names.

"You're not a teacher," Allie warns.

"I know," I say, still feeling giddy.

Allie eyes me, her lids low and squinty. Then she says, "Camp's over, everybody. Rihan, let's go practice free throws."

Rihan hesitates. Just for a second. But then he nods and follows Allie off the porch like an obedient puppy.

What was that?

We were having *fun*. The camp was *working*. And then Allie had to ruin it! She had to be the boss and take over, just because she couldn't guess any of the states. Because she didn't have the spotlight for one minute.

I feel a tiny break inside me, like a bone, only it's somewhere in my chest. Two campers down. This isn't good. At some point in the last hour, I started to realize how lonely I've been. I haven't hung out with a single kid since school got out, and that was weeks ago. I thought it was just Dad I was missing, but it's more than that.

I force myself to smile brightly at Kayla and Lucia. "Don't worry," I tell them, "I have a great idea for what to do next at our new and improved, all-girls camp."

Kayla smiles back. It's the kind where your lips press together and curve up, but your eyes don't smile with them. She stands up and says, "I'm going home for lunch. Thanks, though. I liked the trivia."

As Kayla walks off, I look at Lucia—my lone enthusiastic camper.

"I guess camp's over," I tell her sadly.

"Why?" Lucia asks. "My mom said she hoped it was all day. Isn't it all day?"

"It was supposed to be."

Why did my camp fail? Was it the geography? Or was it *me*?

For a minute, when everyone was trying to remember which states ended in *A*, they were all excited. I felt it. They *wanted* to know the answers. And then—*poof!* It was over.

Lucia points at the clear bin of beads I put on the windowsill and asks if she can make a bracelet.

"Sure," I say, handing her the bin. I open it and show her the new way I learned to knot the thread the other day.

"This is fun," she says as she starts to add beads. "You should run a jewelry camp instead. I bet your sister wouldn't have to make everyone come to that."

Icy pricks cover my body, like I'm being submerged in the freezing waters of the Arctic Ocean Basin.

Not only did no one want to *stay* at my camp—no one wanted to come in the first place. Allie made them.

I thought the kids here were giving me a chance. But no—they just want my sister to like them.

The same thing happened with the neighbors in Fayetteville. At first, everyone was nice to both of us. But then when they got to know us better, it was only Allie they wanted to hang out with.

The tiny break inside me gets bigger and threatens to swallow me up.

This must be how Greenland feels—totally alone, and not really a part of anything.

12

Fact: Studies have shown that heart attacks increase the week after daylight saving time begins. Researchers think the increase is due to the disruption of our internal clock, which doesn't have time to prepare our organs for waking up. Studies also indicate that car accidents increase in the weeks after the start of daylight saving time.

I hide in my room for the next few days. I write emails to Adam, Shuri, and my dad. I do research for my fact cards. I make myself grilled cheese sandwiches and eat them while reading. I do all the things I love to do that I don't have much time for during the school year. But they don't feel as satisfying as they normally would.

Mom works on her big project from early morning until dinner every day. Her bedroom door stays closed. She doesn't seem to notice that my camp's not running or that Dad isn't calling us. If she does notice, she's choosing not to say anything.

My loneliness is palpable. I can't stop thinking to myself how much better things would be if Dad were here with us.

After lunch one day, I decide I need some fresh air. I head outside to the front porch, which is still set up for camp. I sit cross-legged on the swing and carefully color a map of Thailand. I think maps are as beautiful as any art because maps tell the story of a place. Cartographers—professional mapmakers—use colors that are scientifically proven to best convey different types of information. You just have to learn how to read them.

If I were a map, what would my story be? How would the cartographer show how different I am from other kids when I look exactly the same?

"I got you!" Allie yells from across the street. "I got you *twice!*"

She and Rihan are playing Super-Drench squirt guns with the Stein brothers, who live in the mint-green house across the circle. The four of them are chasing each other around, diving under shrubs for cover, getting as filthy as possible. Rihan has ripped his T-shirt, and Allie is covered in mud.

They didn't ask me to play Super-Drench. Maybe Allie assumes I wouldn't want to, or that I'd try to change the rules and mess up the game. Which I probably would. But just once, it would be nice to run around and get soaking wet and not have to *think* about everything, like climate change and rising sea levels and why Hawaii and most of Arizona choose not to follow daylight saving time with the rest of the US.

My brain never stops analyzing the world and everything I know about it. Sometimes it's just plain exhausting.

The older Stein brother howls as Rihan sprays him directly in the face, which apparently counts as a zombie kill in their game. Rihan yells *"Keeee-yah!"* and does a high kick to celebrate.

To my left, three doors down, a screen door bangs shut. Kayla walks onto her porch, ready to paint. I wave at her but she doesn't wave back.

Maybe she doesn't see me. Maybe she does.

Feeling sorry for myself, I open my fact box and remove half of the index cards. I begin to stack them carefully into a pyramid shape, the way people sometimes stack playing cards. Since index cards aren't very stiff, I use them in pairs to make them stronger. It's difficult, precise work and takes all my concentration. The result is impressive. I'm going to call it Khufu, which is the name of the largest pyramid in Egypt.

Out of nowhere, I feel a raindrop on my cheek. Then my ear. Then a huge spray hits my neck. I jump back, and Allie pops up from behind the laurel bushes and soaks me and Khufu.

"Take that, zombie! You'll never get my brains," she yells.

"Stop it, Allie!" I shriek, putting my arms up to shield my face. I watch as my beautiful pyramid starts to wilt, coming dangerously close to collapse. Even worse, the water is blurring all the ink on my cards. "YOU'RE RUINING MY CARDS!"

I sound hysterical, like someone whose brains are actually being eaten by zombies, but I can't help it. I'm upset about the cards, but also about every other thing that's going wrong.

Allie obeys and drops the squirt gun, her mouth open, her eyes wide with surprise. "I wasn't trying to mess up your cards. I just came to ask you to play with us. The Steins had to go somewhere so we have an extra squirt gun you can use."

I double blink my eyes to clear them. Allie and Rihan want me to join them? "Really?" I ask.

"Yeah, really."

Part of me wants to go and play with them. But the other part of me, a much bigger part, wants to do immediate damage control on my cards. My pyramid now has a distinct lean to the left.

"Well?" she says. "Do you want to play or not?"

I want to say yes. I really do. But I know it would end badly and just make things worse between Allie and me. "No, thanks."

Allie shakes her head, like I'm a lost cause, and runs back to the other side of the cul-de-sac. I hurriedly dismantle my pyramid and take my damp cards into the house, where I lay them out on the kitchen counter. Then I run and get the hair dryer from the upstairs bathroom and carefully dry each one. A few cards are ruined, and a bunch more are blurry. I try to guess at the facts written on the ruined ones, but my handwriting is small and the letters have run together.

Before I can stop myself, I'm hollering, *"Mom!"* and running up the stairs to her bedroom.

I push open the door and burst into the room. Mom is hunched over her desk typing, her fingers running a marathon over the keyboard. She doesn't even turn to look at me.

"I'm right in the middle of a thought," she says, holding up one finger. "Hang on."

"But Mom, Allie shot my—"

"Hang on!"

I wait for what feels like forever. Mom's fingers *tappy tap tap*. At last, there are a few clicks of the mouse, and she turns to face me. "It's saved. Now, what's going on? Is anything broken?"

"No, nothing's broken. Well, except a bunch of my fact cards are ruined because Allie shot at them with a Super-Drench gun."

Mom looks disappointed. "What happened to your camp? Weren't you two supposed to be doing that together?"

I guess she did notice my camp didn't work out. I stare down at the carpet and sort of shrug one shoulder. Then I notice her bed, which is unmade on her side. Dad's side looks as neat as if he'd just made it, hospital corners and all.

The image of him on our sofa on a weekend morning, reading the paper in his navy sweatpants and laughing at something with Mom, pops into my head.

DAD. Big, warm, funny Dad, drinking his tea and wearing his glasses.

Come sit, Ginny, he'd say. *I want to read you this article about how you can tell the temperature by counting a cricket's chirps.*

Suddenly my heart feels raw and achy, like my throat when I had strep last year.

"Do you sleep like that?" I ask Mom. "Just on your side, keeping Dad's all neat and tucked in?"

Mom looks at the bed and then at me. She smiles sheepishly.

"You know how your dad loves his hospital corners," she says. "And I hate making the bed. So when he's away, I keep his side neat for him and just let my side be messy."

I feel like she's told me a secret. Something Dad and Allie don't know.

"You miss him terribly," she says.

I nod.

"I'm sorry he hasn't been able to call or email us from the CSH much yet," she says. "It'll get better as he settles in. But in the meantime, it would be good to focus your energy on meeting kids here."

"I've met them," I tell her.

Mom doesn't answer. She just watches me. Quietly. Patiently. The way Dad does when he knows I have something to say but I'm not ready to say it.

"They don't like me," I admit. "They didn't like my camp, or me, or any of it."

"Meeting new people is always hard. Especially if you have a strong personality."

Strong personality? I've never heard myself described that way. Know-it-all, maybe. Supernerd. Brainiac. Teacher's pet.

"It's hard for me sometimes," Mom continues. "I'm too blunt. I hate all that parenting chitchat most moms seem to like. I don't want to talk about the best swim classes, or healthy after-school snacks."

"That does sound boring," I say.

"It is. For me, at least. Anyway, I just read an article about conversation icebreakers that was interesting. Do you want to see it?"

I open my mouth, ready to automatically reply *no*, because I'm not used to talking to Mom like this. I think she's blunt too. So many sharp edges.

But then I think about how boring the last few days have been and say, "I guess so."

Mom picks up a printout from her desk and motions for me to sit down. I perch carefully on the edge of the bed, so I don't mess up Dad's side.

"One icebreaker is called Would You Rather," she says, reading from the article. "You just ask someone a question like, Would You Rather go to sleepaway camp or go to the beach with your family? They answer, and you talk about it some, and then they ask you a question."

"My answer is neither," I say. "I'd rather go to Alaska and experience twenty-four hours of daylight."

Mom laughs. "See? There you go. Great conversation starter. Whomever you were talking to would know that you're very interested in traveling and experiencing the world."

I nod slowly. It's an interesting suggestion. "Do another one," I say.

Mom thinks a second. "Well, with Allie you could ask, Would You Rather hang out with Obi-Wan Kenobi or Luke Skywalker for a day?"

"She'd say Obi-Wan, obviously." We both know the answer to that because Allie has loved Obi-Wan Kenobi since we first saw the Star Wars movies when we were little. But I get Mom's point. You can ask about anything.

"Now you try it," Mom says. "Ask me one."

She settles back in her desk chair, folding her arms and crossing her legs at the ankles.

It's not as easy to come up with a question on my own. "Would You Rather live here or in Fayetteville?"

Mom swats at me with her hand. "No fair! We've only been here a few weeks. Try again, and keep it light, Ginny. We don't need to be serious every second."

I take a deep breath and think harder. "Would You Rather have a triple-scoop ice cream sundae with nuts and hot fudge or two pieces of Grandma's cherry pie?"

Mom laughs. "That's a good one! I think the ice cream sundae. But don't tell Grandma, promise?"

I laugh too. Grandma's cherry pie is good, but not as good as Grandma thinks it is. "I promise."

Mom reaches out for my hand and holds it. She never does things like that—Dad is the affectionate one. But I let her hold my hand for a few seconds before pulling away.

———

After dinner, Allie announces she has another video chat with Mara and takes the tablet upstairs for privacy. I'm envious, as I still haven't heard back from either Adam or Shuri yet.

But just a few minutes later, Allie comes back downstairs.

"You're off already?" I ask.

"Had to reschedule," she says, breezing through the front door and letting it bang behind her.

It's too nice of an evening to be stuck inside again so I follow her out, wondering if there's some way I can accidentally bump into Supriya. I haven't seen her since I went to jewelry camp.

I dawdle on the front porch, watching as Allie grabs her basketball and takes off across the cul-de-sac toward the Steins' house. Jack and Emily, the little twins next door, are riding scooters up and down their driveway. It gives me an idea.

I go to our garage and wrestle my bike out of the corner, where it's been sitting since we moved.

I strap on my helmet and set up the pedals with the right pedal positioned up high so I can get a good push with my foot to start. Then I coast down our driveway and cruise into the cul-de-sac.

I pump my legs, going around and around the circle. The breeze on my face is nice. Being outside on a summer evening when you don't have anything to do or anywhere to be is also nice. It's not like winter evenings when it's cold and you have homework. Something happens as I continue to ride around the circle—the jumping-bean thoughts that are always popping around in my brain settle, and my body settles with them.

I feel so good that I decide to cruise by Supriya's house, which is across the street, the third one before the cul-de-sac. I pedal confidently, raising a hand to wave at little Jack and Emily as I whiz by their driveway.

As I wave, my left hand jerks the handlebars, causing my bike to pitch left, and I fall off the side, into the hydrangeas in Rihan and Supriya's front yard.

There's a sharp pain in my kneecap where it landed on a rock on the ground. I wince as I push myself up on one elbow, telling myself that no one saw me and all I have to do is casually hop back up on the bike and keep going.

Then I hear a door open and feet running toward me.

"Are you okay?" asks Supriya. She's holding a Popsicle, her forehead creased with concern. "I was in the kitchen, and I looked out the window and saw you fly off your bike. Your knee is bleeding!"

I try to decide if this is more embarrassing than when everyone ditched my camp that my sister made them attend, or when I tried to keep my science textbook instead of handing it back in to my teacher and got caught.

I think yes.

"I'm fine," I say, sitting up. "Completely fine."

Supriya narrows her eyes as if she doesn't believe me, then points at the blood oozing down my shin. "You need a Band-Aid. I'll be right back."

She goes inside, and I consider running home to hide in my house. What kind of eleven-year-old can't ride a bike without falling off?

Supriya comes back out with a wet paper towel, a bandage, and a second Popsicle. I clean up my knee, bandage it, and accept the Popsicle.

"Do you want to sit?" she asks. She settles on the top step of her porch, stretching her legs out in front of her. I notice she has on a complicated braided anklet.

"Did you make that at camp?" I ask her.

She nods. "Yeah, yesterday." She looks at me. "There are still two weeks left, you know. Do you think you'll come back?"

I lick my Popsicle, unsure how to say *no way, no chance*, without hurting her feelings. "Maybe."

We sit quietly for a minute.

I want to share a fact so badly I can feel it. It's like holding in a sneeze. But then I remember my conversation with my mom earlier about icebreakers.

A robin flies by, carrying twigs in its mouth. "Would You Rather live in the water or in the sky?" I ask her.

"Hmmm," she says. "I really liked mermaids when I was little, so I'd say water. How about you?"

"Sky," I answer immediately. "I'd love to be a bird and fly over the land and see all the contours and mountains and valleys. I'd go everywhere! I'd fly over the Grand Canyon, the Painted Desert, Yosemite National Park."

Supriya smiles. "Can I change my answer? That sounds pretty fun."

I smile back, feeling happier than I expected. Supriya liked my answer! Unfortunately, my knee has started bleeding through the bandage, so I lie flat on my back and put my leg up over my head.

"What are you doing?" Supriya asks.

"Elevating my leg to stop the bleeding," I explain. "All the blood will flow back to my heart this way, and the cut can clot faster. My dad's a doctor."

"Really? My mom's a dermatologist. What kind is your dad?"

"He's an ER doctor in the Army Medical Corps, but right now, he's deployed to Afghanistan. He left a few weeks ago."

"Wow," Supriya says. "Afghanistan. Can you call him all the time at least?"

It's difficult to talk like this, flat on my back with my leg up in the air. I sit back up and hope my knee stops bleeding on its own.

"Not really—it's hard to get him on the phone and the time change is eight and a half hours. I haven't talked to him since he got there."

"Seriously? I thought with Wi-Fi, you'd be able to talk all the time."

I shrug. That's what everyone thinks. But the mountains of Afghanistan are nothing like the suburbs outside Washington, DC. All the older military families we know say how much easier deployments are now that there's email and video chat. You used to have to wait forever for letters to go back and forth, or the service member had to go stand in line at the phone bank in the MWR (Morale, Welfare, and Recreation) tent and use a phone card to make a call, with tons of people all around listening in. But it's still not *easy*.

"You must miss him a lot," she says. "And you just moved!"

Supriya's genuine sympathy cracks my heart like an egg. I've had Mom telling me for days not to worry, everything's fine, he's just busy. Acting like this is all normal. But I know it's not. Even Supriya knows it.

Suddenly I realize I forgot to scan the headlines this morning to see if there were any attacks on US service members. I've been checking every day. What if it's not the Wi-Fi and something *is* wrong? What if a truck bomb went off, or the CSH got attacked?

"Ginny? You're really pale. Are you okay?"

I look at Supriya and try to focus. "Yeah, I'm fine."

"Is it your knee?"

"Um, yes. It's hurting," I lie.

My mind is racing. The last time Dad deployed, I didn't know enough to worry very much. I just missed him and didn't understand why he wasn't home with us. But it's much worse now that I read the news and know what's going on.

Why isn't he calling me back?

Should I send him an SOS email and tell him I need him to reply urgently? What if he's saving someone's life right this very second? What if he's been awake for three straight days and has barely eaten, like one of the soldiers on the YouTube video I watched?

"You don't look good," Supriya says. "Should I get my mom?"

I shake my head. "I'm not sick. I'm just really worried about my dad."

"Oh." She's quiet for a minute. "You can talk about it if you want."

"Thanks," I say. "But that seems to make it worse. It's better when I'm distracted."

She nods, her expression sympathetic. "Well, in that case, Would You Rather...sit here and have me tell you about this really good mystery I just read, or go home and fix up your knee?"

She did it. She played the Would You Rather game! My heart skips a beat.

"I Would Rather...hear about the book," I say, flashing her a smile. "I've got another knee."

Fact: Africa is home to the world's hottest place year-round (Dallol, Ethiopia); the world's longest river (the Nile); and the world's largest nonpolar desert (the Sahara). It's also home to 30 percent of the world's languages; more than two thousand different languages are spoken on the continent.

The next morning, I'm reading news headlines when I hear my email *ding.* My heart starts racing. I pull up my inbox and see that it's from Dad. Finally!

I stab repeatedly at the screen with my finger to open the email, which causes the screen to freeze. I have to shut down and restart the tablet. By the time I get it on again and open the email, I'm practically sweating.

To: Ginnylovesgeo@gmail.com
From: drjpierce@me.com
Subject: Re: DAD PLEASE REPLY!!!!!!!!!!!!!!!!

Dear Ginny,

I only have five minutes—will write more later! I'm SO sorry about your camp getting canceled. I can imagine how disappointed you must have been. But I LOVE your idea of running your own! How is it going? Who are your campers? What facts are you using? Here's one—did you know the ocean is so vast that some scientists think 91 percent of its species have yet to be discovered? They're just hiding out beneath the water, waiting to be found. Maybe you will find some of them one day.

Write back and tell me ALL about your camp. I'm so proud! Only a little more than five months to go. Love you to the moon (which, as you know, is shaped like a lemon, not a ball).

Dad

I put the tablet down, feeling almost worse than when I picked it up. All that worrying and waiting for days and days. And for what? One short, outdated email? My jewelry camp fiasco was a week ago. Not only that, I can't write him back now, because I'll have to tell him what happened at my camp, and it's embarrassing. He told me to be the glue and to follow my true north, and I'm failing at both of those things.

I turn the tablet off. I can't reply until I have something good to tell him.

I wonder how long that will take.

———————

I'm in my room when I hear Mom talking on the phone. I get up to go see if it could be Dad. But when I reach her door, I realize she's interviewing someone. She's asking questions about the target audience for her piece.

And that's when it hits me. *Interviews!* That's how I could fix my camp. And then I'd have something to write Dad about.

When I want to find out something about Sub-Saharan Africa, I do research, usually in my giant geography textbook or online. For my camp, I need to do a different kind of research: people research.

I've always wanted to conduct interviews. And, of course, real geographers do it all the time when they're doing field research and traveling the world. This will be good practice for me.

I retrieve a stack of blank index cards from my desk and start by creating a card for each kid. I write the same questions on every card. On the *Ginny* card, I fill in my answers, even though I already know them. They'll be the baseline for my research.

GINNY

1. WHAT ARE YOUR HOBBIES? (Studying countries, cultures, and continents)
2. WHERE IS THE FARTHEST YOU'VE EVER TRAVELED? (Tacoma, Washington)
3. WHAT IS SOMETHING YOU'D LIKE TO LEARN? (The gross domestic product, or GDP, of every country)
4. WHAT SUBJECT DO YOU ALWAYS GET AN A IN? (All of them)
5. WHAT WOULD MAKE GEOGRAPHY CAMP FUN FOR YOU? (Enthusiastic campers! New facts! Mapping an unknown place!)

With index cards in hand, I head outside. The sun is bright overhead, shining like a good omen, and I see Lucia doing a series of cartwheels on her front lawn.

"Hi, Lucia," I say, waving.

Lucia lands upright, then immediately hurls herself forward again, this time into a handstand.

"Hi, Ginny!" she yells back as she balances on her hands for several seconds. Her gymnastics skills are impressive.

"Can I interview you?" I ask. "I'm thinking about running my camp again, but this time I want to include activities everyone likes."

"Okay—well, I liked making that bracelet with you. I did not like the trail mix."

"Great, very helpful." I write that on a card. Then I ask her my list of questions, most of which she answers while upside down. Her answers are predictable yet informative.

LUCIA

1. WHAT ARE YOUR HOBBIES? (Cartwheels, handstands, back walkovers)

2. WHERE IS THE FARTHEST YOU'VE EVER TRAVELED? (The beach—Note: Subject does not recall the name of the beach she visited.)

3. WHAT IS SOMETHING YOU'D LIKE TO LEARN? (How to make cookies)

4. WHAT CLASS DO YOU ALWAYS GET AN A IN? (Subject didn't get grades in kindergarten.)

5. WHAT WOULD MAKE GEOGRAPHY CAMP FUN FOR YOU? (Chocolate, ice cream, dress-ups)

"This is really helpful, Lucia, thank you," I say. I tuck her card into my shorts pocket.

One down, three to go. Might as well do the hardest next. I march determinedly toward the basketball hoop, where Rihan and Allie are playing. Allie's ponytail is swinging, and she shoots with complete confidence, even though she's playing against a boy who's several inches taller. Somehow Allie makes hard, athletic things look easy.

"What do you have now?" Allie asks.

"H-O-R," Rihan replies.

Allie whoops. "I've only got H!"

"Are you playing horse?" I ask. "You know, it might be more interesting if you used a different word every time. Like maybe *tundra* or *equator*?"

"Thanks, but I don't think using geography words would make it 'more interesting,'" Allie says.

I shrug. "Just a suggestion. Listen, I want to make my camp better and try it again. All I need is for you both to answer a few questions."

To my surprise, Rihan says, "Yeah, okay."

So I plunge ahead, asking my list of questions and ignoring Allie's occasional beleaguered sigh. I write their answers neatly on my index cards.

<u>ALLIE</u>

1. WHAT ARE YOUR HOBBIES? (Basketball, cross-country, soccer, boogie boarding)
2. WHERE IS THE FARTHEST YOU'VE EVER TRAVELED? (Tacoma, Washington)
3. WHAT IS SOMETHING YOU'D LIKE TO LEARN? (Half-court shot)
4. WHAT SUBJECT DO YOU ALWAYS GET AN A IN? (Note: Subject doesn't answer. Just glares.)
5. WHAT WOULD MAKE GEOGRAPHY CAMP FUN FOR YOU? (No facts. No geography. A miracle.)

<u>RIHAN</u>

1. WHAT ARE YOUR HOBBIES? (Basketball, zombie hunting)
2. WHERE IS THE FARTHEST YOU'VE EVER TRAVELED? (Mumbai, India)

3. WHAT IS SOMETHING YOU'D LIKE TO LEARN? (Tae kwon do)
4. WHAT SUBJECT DO YOU ALWAYS GET AN A IN? (Social studies, math, music)
5. WHAT WOULD MAKE GEOGRAPHY CAMP FUN FOR YOU? (A contest)

"Wow, Rihan, you've been to Mumbai? I would love to go to India! To go anywhere international, really."

He nods. "Yeah, we go every summer to see my grandparents and cousins."

"You're lucky," I say, rereading his answers. So far, his are the most interesting. "Did you know that tae kwon do is an Olympic sport? It originated in Korea, even though some people confuse it with karate, which comes from Japan—"

Allie interrupts me. "Ginny, whenever you start a sentence with 'Did you know,' people automatically tune out."

I look away, resisting the urge to shove Allie. She's obviously telling me to back off from her new friend.

After an uncomfortable silence, Rihan says, "A tae kwon do uniform is called a *dobok*."

The way he says it, it's like he knows it's a gift to me.

"A *dobok*?" I repeat the word so I'll remember it. I love new words.

He nods at me, one side of his mouth pulling up at the corner. It's not a smile exactly, but it's something.

"Ready, Allie?" he says, turning away to shoot the ball.

It's clear that it's time for me to move on. I want to thank Rihan but decide not to do it in front of my sister. She's already annoyed at me. Then I get a truly amazing idea and my mouth opens before I can stop myself.

"Rihan, would you like to prepare a special report on India and present it at my new and improved camp? You could show us pictures from your trips, play Indian music, tell us about the places you've been." I'm so excited about the idea I feel like I've got fifty light bulbs inside me, all lit up.

Rihan's face lights up too—for a second. Then Allie butts in with, "We're not in *school*, Ginny!"

"Let Rihan talk," I snap. "You're not his keeper."

I glance at Rihan, hoping he'll be glad I defended him, but it's like a curtain has come down over his face. He shakes his head and says, "Thanks, but I don't really know that much about India."

He obviously does—he visits every summer and his

relatives live there. Is he refusing to do it because he knows Allie wouldn't approve, or is it like with Supriya, that he doesn't want to be singled out for being Indian?

"You don't have to do a presentation," I tell him. "You could just talk about it a little. Allie and I have never been there, or anywhere in Asia, but our dad is in Afghanistan right now."

"He is?" Rihan looks at Allie, confused.

"Didn't you tell him?" I ask.

Allie shakes her head, all casual, as if she'd merely forgotten to tell Rihan she doesn't like carrots. But it's not casual. It's a big, huge deal. She made a new friend, whom she's hung out with almost every day since we got here, and she didn't mention why our dad is never around?

"Why wouldn't you tell him?" I press.

Allie's cheeks flush. "Because I don't want to talk about it," she says. She holds up the basketball and shoots it one-handed against the backboard. "Now, can you please go and let us finish our game?"

Embarrassed, I avoid looking at Rihan as I turn to go, thinking for the millionth time how different my life would be if Allie and I were more alike.

We're not just opposites. We don't even speak the same language.

Fact: During monsoon season in India, animals sometimes ride on other animals—such as a mouse on the back of a frog—to escape floodwaters.

Allie and Rihan's game starts up again, and within seconds their exuberant shouts and the sound of the bouncing ball fills the court.

I feel my confidence disintegrating, little bits of me flying away, like the cinders from a firepit. I know I should go home and pull myself together. But I haven't talked to Kayla and she's out on her porch right now. I remind myself that I want to have something positive to email Dad about.

"Hi, Kayla!" I call out as I climb her porch steps, hoping not to alarm her this time. "What are you working on?"

She steps back from her painting and gestures toward it, indicating I can look if I want.

It's a different canvas from the other day. Instead of the beautiful ginkgo tree as her subject, this time she's painting a postcard she's clipped to the top of her easel, showing a harbor and boats with white sails.

"Wow—that's beautiful," I say, studying her canvas. She's copied it almost perfectly. "Did you finish the ginkgo tree you were working on?"

She slides her eyes sideways at me. "No. I'm out of yellow paint, remember? Yellow and blue make green."

I do remember. "I'm sorry," I say again.

Kayla doesn't respond and goes back to painting, as if I'm not there watching her. She doesn't seem self-conscious either; she just sweeps her brush across her palette and then starts dabbing blobs of blue on the ocean.

"Uh, would you mind answering a few questions?" I ask. "I'd like to try my geography camp again, but I want to make sure it's fun for everyone this time. If, you know, anyone is willing to try it again."

Without taking her eyes from her canvas, she replies, "Mmm, okay."

<u>KAYLA</u>

1. WHAT ARE YOUR HOBBIES? (Painting, drawing, ceramics)
2. WHERE IS THE FARTHEST YOU'VE EVER TRAVELED? (Quebec, Canada)
3. WHAT IS SOMETHING YOU'D LIKE TO LEARN? (Sculpting)
4. WHAT SUBJECT DO YOU ALWAYS GET AN A IN? (Art, language arts, science)
5. WHAT WOULD MAKE GEOGRAPHY CAMP FUN FOR YOU? (If everyone let me use them as portrait models)

Kayla has also traveled abroad? I wonder if she and Rihan know how lucky they are.

"What's Quebec like?" I ask. I've always found Canada intriguing because there's an area in the Hudson Bay region that has less gravity than the rest of the planet. Dad has promised to take me there one day. "Does it look different from the US?"

Kayla stops moving her brush and actually focuses on me. I make a mental note—this must be something she likes talking about.

"It's nice," she says. "My mom grew up there. Her parents are originally from Martinique, but they moved to Canada when they got married. They all speak French, but all I can say is *oui*, *non*, and *merci*."

"I've never been to another country and I really, really want to go," I say enviously.

"Why do you want to go to another country so badly?" Kayla asks. "What's wrong with here?"

"Nothing, really," I reply quickly. Silver Spring is nice enough from what I've seen. There are parks, neighborhoods with old trees, and big grocery stores. It's a lot like the other places Dad has been stationed.

Maybe that's what's missing—the places we've lived are all kind of the same.

"I guess I'd like to go somewhere completely different," I tell her. "My dad is deployed to Afghanistan, and the last time he came back from a tour, he had these amazing things to show us: clothing, spices, food. And my mom said even *he* seemed different."

"Different how?"

I hadn't remembered Mom saying that until just now—that Dad was different the last time he came home. Does that mean he'll be different this time too?

Will things be the same between us when he's back?

That hadn't even occurred to me, that things might not be the same when he returns in December. I feel that tiny break in my chest again, like a wishbone snapping, and suddenly I want to crawl under a porch chair and hide. Why did I start talking about Dad?

"He was different how?" Kayla asks again.

"I don't remember," I say. "I was in first grade at the time....My mom said I stopped talking about him after a month or two...."

Other memories from his last deployment are coming back to me now. The videos he sent of him reading books to us. And how I didn't like to watch them because I couldn't interrupt and ask questions the way I did when he was at home.

Why couldn't I remember any of this before? Did my brain make me forget on purpose?

"Are you okay?" Kayla asks. She lays her brush down on the easel tray. "Want to sit down or something?"

"No, thanks." The last thing I need is to fall apart on Kayla's porch. "I'm just...hungry, I guess. Thanks for your interview answers."

I grab my index cards and hurry off the porch, making a beeline back to my house.

I pass Jack and Emily playing in the sandbox in their

front yard. Jack whacks Emily in the shoulder with a bucket, and she yells, "STOP IT, STINKER."

I wave at them but keep moving. I scurry through my front door and up to my room.

Now the memories from the last deployment are pouring in like a flood. I remember how hard it was to get a hold of him. How Mom would say that Dad could always reach *us*, but we had to have all the stars aligned to reach *him*. And how Mom would keep a list of things she wanted to tell him posted to the fridge, so she wouldn't forget. And then sometimes she'd just throw the list away after a few days because by the time she'd get the chance to tell him, it had happened days ago, and it hardly mattered anymore.

I remember playing with my dollhouse, and Mom handing me her cell phone with Dad on video chat. I'd hold the phone with his face on it like it was one of my dolls and move it around in the dollhouse as I played, with Dad doing some of the doll voices.

My brain tells me that Dad is fine—I just got an email from him this morning. But my fear says *That was hours ago. Anything can happen. He's in a war zone.*

I pick up the tablet on my bed and try to call him. It rings and rings but no one answers. When the voice mail

clicks on, I say, "Dad, it's Ginny. *Please* call me the minute you get this. I need to hear your voice. I miss you.
Are you being careful? Please call me. Okay? I love you."

The inside of my nose is tingling. Tears leak out of
my eyes. I scan the news headlines, reading just enough
to scare myself. Ten minutes go by. Twenty. Thirty. He
doesn't call.

I hug the tablet to my chest and curl up on my side. I
thought things would be getting easier by now. Instead,
they're getting worse.

How am I going to make it until December?

Fact: All giant pandas in the world, no matter where they're born, are owned by China. The use of giant pandas as diplomatic gifts to other countries is called panda diplomacy, and dates back to the Tang dynasty in the seventh century.

I don't hear back from Dad. With nothing else to distract me from worrying, I decide to throw myself into preparations for Ginny's Camp Part II. I spend the rest of the weekend coming up with new ideas based on my interviews, hoping that this time my camp will be something everyone *wants* to come to.

On Monday morning, I grab my last clean pair of shorts and tiptoe downstairs to begin getting ready. I want to get as much done as possible before anyone else gets up.

I start by toasting a bagel and setting the oven to preheat. Then I open the fridge and pull out the roll of chilled sugar cookie dough I made yesterday. My camp promised facts and snacks last time, and my snacks were terrible. Luckily, this is an easy problem to fix. I love to bake.

I cover the cutting board with flour to keep the dough from sticking and start rolling it out. Allie and I always decorate sugar cookies at Christmas, but we do them in the shapes of trees and wreaths and angels. These will be better.

Once I have a thin, even layer of dough, I grab a plastic knife and begin to carve it into continent shapes. Africa and South America look somewhat similar, but South America is skinnier and pointier on the bottom.

As I'm carefully carving a Europe, Mom appears in her pajamas and starts the coffee maker.

She looks at the huge slab of dough on the counter and the blinking oven light. As if it knows it'll get me in trouble, the oven beeps that it's finished preheating.

Mom exhales heavily. "You know you're not supposed to use the oven by yourself."

"I know, but I've decided to give my camp another try, and I need to have something delicious to offer my campers," I tell her. "So I figured I'd make cookies. And look—I'm molding them in the shapes of continents."

I show her my best Europe. Her frown relaxes as she examines my work. "That's really good, Ginny. You have excellent marketing instincts. Maybe you should be doing my project instead of me."

Excellent instincts? *Me?* I've never thought my instincts were good. They always seem to lead me in the wrong direction.

"Thanks, Mom," I say. "Do you think the kids will like them?"

She nods. "I do, yes. So *just this once* I won't yell at you about the oven, but I'm going to put in the cookie sheets for you. Deal?"

"Deal." I hand her the two pans I've already filled with continent cookies, and she slides them in.

As the coffee percolates, Mom checks emails on her phone, and I carve out another batch of cookies. I probably have enough already, but they're so satisfying to make I can't stop.

"Anything from Dad?" I ask.

"Nooooo," Mom says, not lifting her eyes from her phone. "I'll always tell you when I hear from him, okay?"

I nod, my vision going blurry. I blink the tears away and try to focus on carving my dough.

"I left him a voice mail two days ago saying I was worried about him and to please reply ASAP. And he hasn't emailed or called since!"

Mom moves to stand beside me. She puts her hand over mine. "No news is usually good news during deployments. We'd know if something was wrong."

Her words are calm and rational. But her face tells a different story. It's puffy, and there are dark circles under her eyes.

"You look tired," I say. "Didn't you go to bed early last night?"

Mom bristles, clearly offended. "No, I was trying to get some work done."

I don't ever remember Mom working at night before— especially on a Sunday. Sunday evenings are family time. When Dad was here, we'd have an early dinner and movie night, or go out for ice cream, or take a walk.

"You're working a lot more than usual," I say.

The coffee maker beeps that it's finished. Mom opens a cabinet and chooses an extra-large mug.

"Yes, I am," she replies. "It helps me. Just like I think camp will help you."

"Camp isn't enough to make me stop missing Dad and worrying about him."

"I know that," she says, more gently. "But it will get easier. The beginning is the hardest part, and we're almost through the first month. Pretty soon it'll start to feel normal."

"I don't *want* this to feel normal."

Mom sighs and wraps her arm around me. She rests her chin on my head and gives me a squeeze. "Of course you don't. Neither does he. But life is what we make of it, right? You can be as happy or as miserable as you allow yourself to be."

"I guess."

Mom smiles. "You are so much like him, you know."

"I am?" I say, surprised. "But Dad is perfect!"

She laughs. "First of all, nobody's perfect. And second, you've only known him as an adult. He had his own challenges as a kid. Everyone does."

"Allie doesn't. And I bet you didn't."

"Don't assume you know what other people are dealing with. Allie is a lot more complicated than you think she is."

"Complicated how?" I ask. "Everything is easy for her. We've only been here a few weeks and the kids in the neighborhood follow her around everywhere."

"That isn't everything," Mom says, just as her phone alarm beeps. She picks it up and reads the screen. "Shoot—I have a call with the client in five minutes." She grabs her mug and smooths her hair back. "I've got to log on. Sorry, Ginny."

I turn my back to get the cooling racks from the cupboard, so Mom won't see how disappointed I am. She and I never have talks like this, and now she can't even stay to finish it?

"We'll talk more later, okay?" Mom says. "Good luck with your camp!" She races back upstairs and closes her door.

Mom won't care who puts the cookies in the oven now, so I slip on a pair of oven mitts to remove the first batch and slide in the second. They smell and look great, but they've lost some of their magic. I wish Mom had stayed to talk to me the way Dad would have. And what did she mean about Allie being more complicated than I think she is? I've known Allie my entire life.

I need you, Dad. WHERE ARE YOU?

I pick up an Asia cookie, calculating where Afghanistan would be. Then I crumple it up in my fist and toss it in the trash.

※※———※※

While the cookies cool, I plunk down at the kitchen table to work on new flyers. I could go tell the other kids face-to-face, but the flyers will help me avoid any awkward conversations about what went wrong last time.

Enjoy FEWER FACTS and BETTER SNACKS
at Ginny's NEW and IMPROVED Geography Camp!
Today at 11:00 am
Ginny's front porch
It's Still Fun! It's Still FREE!
ONLY NOW IT'S BETTER!
(No quizzes! No homework!
Lots of GAMES!)

Once the cookies are ready, I decorate them with sprinkles and icing to indicate mountain ranges and bodies of water. They're not as accurate as I'd like, but I taste test a North America, and it's delicious.

Allie is still asleep, so I creep upstairs and slide my new flyer under her door. Across the hall, I can hear Mom's fingers clacking away on her keyboard.

I head outside to deliver the rest of the flyers. No one is playing yet, so I push them beneath their front doors and hope it's the first thing they see when they come down for breakfast.

As I look around my camp headquarters, I realize I should make the porch more comfortable. I lower the wooden shade at the far end to block the sun from the south, so it'll be cooler when we're sitting out here. Then I retrieve an old standing fan from our garage and plug it in on one side of the porch. I find a box of decorations left over from various family birthday parties and blow up the balloons and string up the streamers, so the porch looks like a party. I fluff up the cushions on the chairs and sweep a few dead moths off the windowsills.

Standing at one end of the porch, I look at my new setup. It's much more festive than last time. It looks cool and shady, but with a party atmosphere. Who wouldn't want to sit here later, when the sun will be hot, and everyone will be thirsty and need a break from playing outside?

Maybe Mom is right. Maybe I do have good marketing instincts.

I go back inside and mix up a large pitcher of lemonade with some of Mom's diet lemonade mix. As I do, my mind wanders to Dad and the heat in Afghanistan. A million questions suddenly occur to me. Does he get to drink lemonade? Does he have cookies? Fans? Air-conditioning?

Why didn't I think to ask him any of these things before he left?

Why didn't I ask if he was scared to go?

Fact: Villa Las Estrellas, one of the few settlements in Antarctica, requires all long-term inhabitants, including children, to have their appendix removed, as there are no specialist surgeons on base.

At eleven o'clock, I sit on our front porch steps watching Allie play street hockey in the cul-de-sac with Rihan. I haven't seen Kayla anywhere, and Lucia was in her yard a while ago but disappeared.

No one seems to notice me. It's possible I did all this work—the interviews, the new plans, the cookies and porch decorations—for nothing.

I make myself wait until ten minutes past eleven so I don't seem too anxious. But then I can't wait anymore. I walk over to the old schoolhouse bell hanging beside our front door. No one has rung it since we moved in.

CLANG! CLANG! ***CLANG!***

It's so loud I worry I might go deaf, but I keep ringing it anyway because I like the sound and the feeling of ceremony.

"Camp is starting!" I holler. "Camp!"

Allie's sigh is visible even from across the court. She flicks the puck with her stick, taking a shot at the goal. She misses, and Rihan retrieves the puck, moving into position so he can shoot next.

Just then, I hear a door open to my left and see Lucia bounding out of her house and running at full speed across the lawns to my porch.

At least I'll have one camper.

"I'm so glad you're doing this again!" she says, checking out the new decorations. "Can I have that pink balloon?"

I quickly unstick the balloon from its spot on the streamer and hand it to her, pleased my hard work has made her happy.

"Are the lemonade and cookies for me too?" she asks.

I'm proud of my snacks. They really do look delicious. "For all the campers, yes."

"Yay! My mom won't let me have lemonade except for birthday parties because it's too sugary, but you won't tell, right?"

"I won't tell."

Allie and Rihan continue to play hockey and ignore me. I look at Lucia, happily snapping the end of her balloon, and have an idea.

"Lucia, do you want to go get Kayla?" I ask her. "I'm not sure she heard the bell."

"Sure!" Lucia says, seeming pleased to have a job to do. "I'll be right back."

She bolts off the porch and heads to Kayla's house. I watch as she knocks and waits for the door to open. When I see Kayla in the doorway looking at me over Lucia's head, I wave at her. She waves back limply.

Lucia and Kayla talk awhile, and Kayla keeps looking over at my porch.

At long last, the girls start walking toward me. On the way, they stop in the center of the cul-de-sac, where Lucia starts talking to Allie and Rihan. Even with her loud voice, they're too far away for me to hear her.

All four of them look up at our porch, studying it intently. And then I hear Lucia say, "Lemonade and cookies."

A minute later, my porch is full of campers. *Better snacks!* seems to be a crucial part of running a successful camp.

"Thanks for coming again, everybody," I say, grabbing the cookie plate and handing it to Lucia first since she was so helpful. "Please have a cookie. They're very special shapes, as you can see."

Lucia takes one and holds it up. "It's shaped like a turtle!"

"Not quite," I tell her. "These are continent cookies—that one's Europe."

Kayla takes one and holds it up to show me. "Australia, right?"

I nod. "Yep."

"They smell good," Allie says, grabbing two. She eats them quickly without bothering to identify which continents they are. "Mmm—they taste good too."

The compliments give me such a boost of confidence I almost feel taller.

My cookies seem to have magic powers. Everyone is munching and drinking lemonade and looking content.

"We're not going to do any school-type work this time," I begin. "We'll just play some games."

Everyone still seems interested. No one is talking over me or looking away or elbowing someone else.

I grow another inch taller. "I was thinking that first we'd play a version of TV tag, only instead of naming a

TV show to get unfrozen, you have to name a European capital city."

I'm pretty pleased with this idea. Everyone loves to tag people out.

"Nice try, but none of us know any European capitals," Allie says.

"I know the capital of England," says Rihan. "It's London. But that's it."

"And Paris, France," adds Kayla. "Everyone knows *that* one."

"Obviously, I know *those*," Allie says, her cheeks red. She glares at me.

I should have known European capitals aren't her thing.

"How about state capitals in the US, then?" I suggest. "That's much easier."

Allie looks away, her face still flushed. But Kayla nods and looks happier. Rihan shrugs, and Lucia takes another cookie.

"What's a state capital?" she asks.

"It's the center of government for each state in our country," I explain. "You know how a state has a governor and a legislature to make its rules? They do that in the state capital."

"Sure," she says.

I don't think she gets it, though.

"How about this?" I say. "I'm going to write down a bunch of state capitals right now, and we'll all study them for a few minutes and then we'll play. Okay?"

"Yeah, okay," says Rihan.

"Do you want me to list them in alphabetical order by city or by state?" I ask. "I taught myself both ways as an independent study project at my old magnet school. I also know all their populations."

"Write them any old way," Allie mutters, just as Rihan says, "What kind of magnet school?"

"It was science themed," I reply. I begin writing the list alphabetically by city.

"That's cool," Rihan says. "My sister goes to a math and science magnet. Are you going to one here?"

"Yes, but I don't know which one yet," I tell him. "I applied late because of our move, so I'm still waiting to get my admissions letter."

I finish writing up the list of states and capitals.

Lucia points at the list, saying, "I can't read all those captions."

"Capitals," I correct her. "How about I write a few on your hand to use for the game?"

I lean over and write several short ones like Dover (Delaware), Saint Paul (Minnesota), and Salem (Oregon) on the back of her hand, and then whisper them in her ear in case she can't read them easily.

"Is everybody ready to play?" I ask.

Kayla hops up. "I'll try it," she says.

Lucia nods and looks happy too. "Yeah, let's play!"

We all head out to the cul-de-sac. Allie is still acting reluctant, like she has better things to do, but Rihan seems to be going along with it.

"NOT IT!" both of them yell as we reach the center of the court. Kayla rolls her eyes, and Lucia looks disappointed. She's probably the slowest, so she doesn't want to be It.

"I'll be It," I tell everyone. "Ready, set, go!"

Everyone begins running. I nab Lucia first because she's so close. She freezes. I see her staring at the words on her hand, trying to sound them out.

I go after Rihan next, but he's extremely fast. Probably from chasing invisible zombies all the time. I zip around, running behind mailboxes and dancing around parked cars, trying to get him. I feel someone run behind me and whirl around to tag Kayla.

"Gotcha!" I yell.

Kayla looks annoyed, but yells "Annapolis," which is Maryland's capital. And then she's unfrozen and off and running again.

"Remember, everybody—you can't repeat a capital," I yell. "Once it's been used, it's out."

The game goes on for a while, with Lucia continually yelling "Salami" instead of "Salem" to unfreeze herself. Allie offers to be It at one point because she's so fast she wants to prove she can get everyone out in two seconds. She gets me immediately, but now that everyone has said most of the easy capitals, I'm the only one who can remember the hard stuff, like Jefferson City (Missouri) and Cheyenne (Wyoming).

We play until everyone is hot and sweaty and we've named almost all fifty capitals. Lucia found a hiding spot in the bushes and missed half the game until Rihan noticed her and tagged her.

"I need more lemonade," she says, gasping, so we all go onto the shady porch and switch on the fan. I go in the house and quickly mix up another pitcher of lemonade.

When I come back out, Lucia is at the easel, drawing all over the blank map of Europe I hung up. I was planning to have a contest to see who could identify the countries the fastest.

I suck in a breath. It's painful watching her draw all over one of my maps. She doodles a flower over Poland and something that looks like a dog bone over the Czech Republic.

I grab my fact box and flip through, hoping I can find a fact that will dazzle my campers.

This is my moment.

Fact: The Ring of Fire is a roughly 25,000-mile path along the Pacific Ocean that outlines the edges of several tectonic plates. It's the site of 75 percent of the world's volcanoes and 90 percent of its earthquakes.

I'm so impatient to impress everyone that I read the first fact I come across.

"Did you guys know the Czech Republic has more castles than any other country in Europe? There are nine hundred thirty-two, including Prague Castle, which is one of the largest in the world."

I look around, hoping for a positive reaction. Instead, Rihan yawns. Allie finishes a third cup of lemonade.

"You promised fewer facts," she reminds me, pointing at the flyer I taped to the porch pillar. She opens her eyes extra wide at me as if to signal that I need to knock it off with the facts.

"I know—I'm just mentioning this one because Lucia is drawing on Prague, so it made me think of it."

I notice Kayla watching me. She looks thoughtful. When I finish speaking, she gets up and stands beside Lucia. "Can I use the easel for a minute?" she asks.

Lucia hands Kayla the purple marker. Kayla grabs another of my blank map copies, flips it around, and clamps it to the easel.

"We're going to play Pictionary," she announces.

She starts drawing. First something that looks like Canada, and then changes, and suddenly it's a baseball field. Kayla adds a few tiny players, then points to the one on the mound.

"Pitcher!" says Allie.

Kayla smiles. "Yes!" She caps the marker and hands it to Allie, indicating she should go next.

"Why'd you draw a *pitcher*?" I grumble, thinking that not only were her picture and clue way too obvious, it doesn't have *anything* to do with what we were discussing, which was Europe. I could draw a flower and everyone could guess it, but so what?

"I love baseball," she says. "And my dad is taking me and Jerome to a Nationals game on Sunday."

My dad is taking me. Her words cut like a knife. The rotating fan passes over me for a second, which is good, because I've just started sweating.

Why isn't Dad calling me back?

"If we're going to play Pictionary," I say, struggling to keep my voice steady, "we should do it the right way. We'll make two teams, and each team can write down words for the other team. Then the drawer picks one for their team to guess."

"I know how Pictionary works," Kayla says. "But everyone was bored, and you were reading facts to us, so *I* came up with something better to do."

She sounds offended, like she'd genuinely tried to help me and I wasn't appreciative. Maybe she's right.

Kayla gestures at Allie. "Your turn."

"Wait!" I say. "You're right—Pictionary is a good idea. Just give me one sec. Please."

Hurriedly, I tear another map printout into small strips of paper and begin writing down place names: *Paris, Australia, San Francisco, Cape Canaveral, Iceland, Siberia.* I fold them up so you can't see what's written inside and arrange them on the empty cookie plate.

"Here," I say to Allie. "Pick one and draw it. They're all place names."

Kayla sits down, still looking offended. Allie looks just plain bored.

"It'll be fun," I promise. I'm half-expecting Allie to say no and start drawing a basketball court, but I guess she can't think of something she wants to draw on her own, because she plucks one of the papers off the plate.

She reads it and nods. Then she starts drawing, and right away I'm pretty sure it's a bear of some kind. But I don't say anything because I want everyone else to have a chance.

She adds ears and a big round belly, and then starts to add blobs of color on the bear. It looks like a panda bear to me because it has one dark eye patch, but it's in purple marker.

After a minute, Rihan says, "Panda bear?"

Allie gets really excited and starts motioning for everyone to keep guessing.

Rihan tries again. "Panda? Panda baby? Big bear? Bamboo?"

"Remember the answer is a place name," I remind everyone, wondering what name she could have, since I wrote them myself, and I didn't put Washington, DC, or any Chinese cities in the pile. Although maybe it's not a panda.

"China," says Kayla, almost immediately. "Shanghai. Beijing. Guangzhou."

Now I'm really curious. What is Allie's clue? Did she make up her own?

Allie keeps pointing at the panda and making big gestures with her hands, like she's picking and eating bamboo, which I don't think is allowed in Pictionary. It isn't charades.

Lucia says, "Hamburgers?"

"Good guess," I tell her encouragingly. If it were hamburgers, it could be Hamburg, Germany, and that would be funny. But that's not it.

This goes on for a few more minutes, with Rihan and Kayla making a lot of good guesses about China and pandas and bamboo and all kinds of things.

Frustrated, Allie asks, "Do you give up?"

"YES," yells everyone except me.

She puts down her marker. "It's Australia!" she says, sitting down and shaking her head like we're all stupid. "That's where pandas live."

Kayla stares at her, perplexed, and Rihan looks away,

toward his house. Lucia seems unaware of Allie's mistake.

"Allie, giant pandas live in *China* and eat bamboo," I inform her. "You're thinking of *koala* bears. They live in Australia and eat eucalyptus."

There's a moment of total silence. Then Allie's face turns a fierce, fiery red. She takes the purple marker and snaps it in half, ink shooting out all over her shirt.

"You know what, Ginny?" she says. "Your camp *sucks*. And if it weren't for me, no one would have even come."

I don't move or speak. I just stare at her, stunned.

"Whoa, Allie," says Rihan. "Chill out."

But Allie can't chill out. She's erupting. "You think you're so great because you go to fancy magnet schools, and you and Dad have your little smart club together. Well, guess what? You're *not* great. You suck even more than your camp."

She storms off the porch and hops on her bike, taking off in the direction of the main road.

Allie has never yelled at me like that in her life. We get mad at each other, and we argue, but she's never been outright *mean*.

My campers sit motionless, waiting for me to do

or say something. My mind spins like the little rainbow wheel on the computer, trying to process what just happened.

"Are you okay?" Kayla asks.

I nod, even though the answer is *no*. I'm definitely not okay.

She sighs, then says in a teachery voice, "You shouldn't have been so mean about the koalas."

Me? Mean to *Allie*?

"You embarrassed her," she says.

I stare back at Kayla, unable to reply. I feel like all the little files of information in my brain are shifting and moving around, trying to sort through what happened. I've never understood why Allie can't remember simple things, like the difference between panda bears and koala bears or where Idaho is located. I always assumed she just didn't care enough to bother.

I guess I did embarrass her. I didn't intend to. But she *humiliated* me.

"You should go apologize," Kayla suggests.

Rihan shakes his head. "I think Allie wants to be alone right now," he says, sounding somewhat possessive, as if after just a few weeks of being Allie's sidekick he knows her better than I do.

"Allie's fine, everybody," I snap. "She's always fine. No matter how often we move, or where we go, she fits right in."

One of the files in my brain shifts again, and I get a flash of Allie back at the ice cream place in Fayetteville, when Dad told us about the deployment. How lost she looked. And how sad she seemed when we were packing up our garage.

How she's been sleeping in that same old Tar Heels shirt almost every night, and won't even wear the Terps shirt Dad gave her as a moving present.

I whirl on Kayla. "You know, you started this with your Pictionary idea!"

"Me?" she says, surprised. "I was trying to help you. You should be thanking me."

"Yeah? Well, I'm *not*."

It's like some other person has taken control of my mouth and is spouting mean things.

Looking uncomfortable, Rihan stands up. "I'm going to go find Allie."

I watch him walk away, feeling a surge of jealousy that this almost stranger has a relationship with my sister that I don't. She wouldn't even want me looking for her.

Lucia picks up my bin of plastic beads sitting on the windowsill and starts sorting through them.

Kayla moves over to sit beside her. "I can show you how to do a pattern if you want," she offers.

"Sure!" says Lucia. "Thanks."

I stare at them, so cozy on the swing together, and feel even more alone. I thought Lucia might like me at least.

"Aren't you guys going to ditch my camp too?" my mean mouth asks them.

Lucia blinks at me. Kayla whispers to her, "How about you come to my house? I have a bunch of beads. I'll show you how to make an anklet if you want."

Lucia nods, and they get up to leave. Lucia looks back at me with injured eyes as they walk off, which makes me feel worse.

I'm left all alone, the ruins of my camp surrounding me like my very own Pompeii.

18

Fact: Australia is the only continent without an active volcano. I wonder if it feels bad about that, like it doesn't fit in with the other continents.

With my camp abandoned yet again, I head inside, slamming the door behind me.

I run through the house looking for the tablet, but it's not in any of its usual spots. As I'm searching under my bed, I realize there's one place I haven't looked. I barge into Allie's room, confident that she won't be back anytime soon.

The room is a mess, with dirty clothes and sneakers covering the floor, and a pile of rolled-up posters in the corner. Allie hasn't hung anything on the walls yet except for one picture that's taped up over her desk. It's of her and Mara, their arms around each other's shoulders and their tongues sticking out.

They look more like sisters than Allie and I do. Their hair color, their slouchy postures and silly expressions.

I stare at the picture for a moment, feeling envious that there's something between Allie and Mara that doesn't exist between Allie and me.

The tablet is on Allie's bed so I grab it and carry it back to my room with me. Hurriedly, I try to call Dad and this time, it goes straight to voice mail. It doesn't even ring. What does that mean? Is he out of battery? No service?

I leave him a semi-hysterical message, telling him to call me back immediately. Then I check my email and my heart leaps.

To: Ginnylovesgeo@gmail.com
From: drjpierce@me.com
Subject: Re: DAD PLEASE REPLY!!!!!!!!!!!!!!!

My dear Ginny,

Why haven't you written me back? I want to hear all about your camp! I bet it's fantastic. How are Mom and Allie? Please write me a long reply and tell me everything. I miss you and love you.

Did you know that Singapore has a building
inspired by the Sandcrawler from *Star Wars*?
Tell your sister.

Love,
Dad

I reread the email several times, relieved to have proof that he's alive and well.

I click *reply*, anxious to tell him everything, but before my fingers can start typing, I pause. It's jarring to have Dad be so out of step with my life. The time stamp on his email says it was written just minutes ago—right when Allie and I were fighting.

Why didn't he mention my two frantic voice mails? Why isn't he telling me anything about *his* daily life? Is something horrible going on there that I can't know about? His email feels superficial and phony.

Is that how I'm supposed to write back, with rosy details and no actual ugly truths?

If I tell him Allie and I are being awful to each other, and my camp was a two-time failure, and Mom is totally checked out, and our house is a pigsty, he'll be upset and worried about us. And I don't want that.

I can't see Dad or talk to him, and now I can't even email him honestly. How is anyone supposed to live like this?

Frustrated, I close my email and toss the tablet onto my bed. I stomp down to the kitchen, hoping to find something to eat and distract myself. I open the fridge and check the deli drawer for lunch meat, but it's all gone. There's no cream cheese or peanut butter either. But there is the packet of bacon I made Mom buy the other day.

I'm not allowed to make it without supervision, but there's nothing else for me to eat. Before I can talk myself out of it, I grab a skillet and place it on the stove, coat it with cooking spray, and lay the strips horizontally across the pan. Within minutes, the bacon is sizzling and the kitchen smells like Dad is home. It makes my heart sing and hurt at the same time.

Using Dad's special bacon tongs, I carefully flip each piece. There's no way I'm going to eat sixteen slices of bacon by myself, but that's okay. Someone will eat them.

When the slices have cooked through, I turn off the burner and transfer them to a plate, where I blot them with paper towels to soak up the grease. I didn't know I could make bacon by myself, but I guess I watched Dad do it enough times to learn how.

I put a few slices between pieces of white toast with some butter and tomato and sit down to eat my sandwich, feeling immensely proud of myself. The bacon is well done and crispy—just like Dad's.

I've barely taken two bites when I hear feet coming down the stairs. Mom calls out, "Do I smell *bacon*?"

"Um, no," I lie.

Mom appears in the doorway. She looks around, taking in the dirty skillet, the greasy paper towels on the counter, and the sink full of dishes from this morning that no one loaded into the dishwasher. Even the kitchen table where I'm sitting is covered in crumbs and sticky patches of jelly.

"Is it too much to ask that you follow the house rules? Put your dishes in the dishwasher. Clean up after yourself!"

Her voice rises with each grievance.

"Sorry. I'll clean up after I eat."

"Gah!" Mom yells. She examines the food spatters on the top of the stove, then picks up one of the greasy paper towels and waves it in the air. "This house is a *mess*.

You and Allie don't help with anything. Have you *noticed* that I'm *busy?*"

My whole body goes rigid and tingly. I hate when Mom gets angry.

"I'm just *one person*, Ginny. I can't do all of this!"

A single salty tear drips down my cheek. I look away so Mom won't see my face.

"I'm sorry," Mom says, sounding defeated.

I don't want her stupid apology. I just want Dad. I would go live with him in Afghanistan if I could.

"I'm exhausted," Mom continues. "This deadline, and trying to keep after everything around the house…"

She tries to lay her hand on my shoulder but I shrug it off.

"*No*," I say firmly.

Mom's cell phone rings, and she fumbles while trying to pull it out of her pocket. It drops to the floor. I hurriedly pick it up and hand it to her.

"I don't know this number," she mumbles. She sounds nervous. "H-hello?"

She exhales, then pauses while someone speaks.

"Is it Dad?" I ask.

She waves a hand and shakes her head no. "You what?" she says. "Oh. Okay. Well, sure, I guess. If you want. Don't you want to come home and get your stuff? Okay. Yeah. Bye."

She hangs up and sinks down into the chair across from me. "It was just Allie. Rihan's parents want to take them to some water park and then out to dinner. I asked her if she wants to grab a bathing suit and towel but I guess his sister is loaning her a suit."

My jealousy is swift and powerful. Supriya is going to the waterpark too?

Allie already has a new best friend, and now she has an invitation to something really fun, *and* the only girl I've liked here is probably going to end up being *her* friend because of Rihan. Supriya and Allie are closer in age too.

I feel another tear on my cheek but I wipe it off.

Mom picks up a piece of bacon and munches on it. "Wow—that's delicious," she says. "You did this yourself?"

I don't respond. She's only being nice because she feels bad for yelling at me.

"What happened this morning?" Mom asks. "I heard you running around outside, and it sounded like it was going well. Did you try the Would You Rather game?"

"No, that game is dumb," I tell her. "That stuff doesn't work." I squeeze my remaining sandwich half into a ball, even though it tastes good and I want to eat it. I smash the bread ball down onto my plate. "And my camp was awful. Nobody here wants to talk to me or hang out with me."

Mom looks taken aback. "That's too bad. I had another idea you might try...."

"I don't want any more of your *ideas*!"

"Fine, then," Mom says. Her voice is steady, but she's clearly hurt. She gets up, shoving her chair back so it screeches on the floor, and takes my plate even though I'm still flattening my sandwich.

She carries the plate to the sink and starts noisily cleaning up the stack of dishes from this morning.

I feel terrible. I lied to her and made her feel bad, when the truth is I liked the game she suggested. Even more, I liked that she'd made an effort to understand me.

I should help her clean up the kitchen. I tell my body to get up, get *moving*. Stop sitting and waiting for some magic fairy dust to appear and make me able to play games the way everyone else does and not try to show off how smart I am.

But my body doesn't move. It's given up.

***

Later, in my room, I stare at myself in the mirror. I look the same as most other people. I'm average height and weight. My features aren't too big or too small. My ears stick out a little, like Dad's. But I'm not the same at all.

I'm wearing my *I have a black belt in geography* T-shirt that was a birthday gift from my grandparents. They must have thought it was funny. I did too, at the time.

I rip it off and toss it into the back corner of my closet. I pull out a plain grass-green T-shirt from my dresser. The color reminds me of an African savanna, a grassland with scattered trees. The most famous one is the Serengeti Plain of Tanzania.

"The Serengeti is home to the world's greatest migration of land animals," I say out loud to no one. "It's one of the seven natural wonders of Africa."

I ache to discuss the Serengeti with someone who cares. Or even someone who will just *listen*.

I grab the tablet from my bed and try for the zillionth time to call Dad, but it goes straight to voice mail again. Why isn't it ringing like it normally does?

I read online the other day about a woman who got a call from her deployed husband, and while they were on the phone, there was a huge boom sound in the background, and her husband said, "Honey, I love you, but I have to go," and hung up. Then she didn't hear from him for two whole weeks. That entire time, his family had to wait and trust that he was all right.

This is not okay. How do other military families do this over and over again?

They fake their way through it, I guess. Just like Dad's fake, phony email to me earlier.

I open my inbox and write him an email similar to the one he sent me. I tell him I love him, but every other word is a lie.

Dear Dad,

Sorry I haven't written! I've been so busy. Things are going great! My camp is wonderful, and I've made so many new friends in the neighborhood. All the kids love learning about

geography and keep asking me for more facts.
I came up with a bunch of cool games that
we've been playing, and the weather is nice so
we're outside all day just hanging out together.

Allie and Mom are awesome too. We are all
doing terrific.

I love you!
Ginny

Fact: At the equator, the speed of the earth's spin is about one thousand miles per hour. We don't feel it because everything—us, the oceans, and the atmosphere—is spinning at the same speed.

I'm already in bed by the time Allie gets home, and the next morning when I get up, she's still asleep. I wonder when we're going to talk about our huge fight during Pictionary yesterday. Will we pretend it didn't happen?

I try to keep my mind busy, reading news headlines and working on a map of the Serengeti. In the key, I include some of the animals that live there, like pangolins, which are the world's only scaly mammal.

Like me, they're noticeably different than their peers. However, pangolins are prized. They're considered vital to the ecosystem, because just one pangolin can eat seventy million ants and termites a year.

In the kitchen, I find a can of tomato soup in the pantry and start heating it up in a pot on the stove. Normally I'd use the microwave, but now that I've been using the stove, I prefer it. I whisk in milk and a dash of Worcestershire sauce, which is how Dad makes tomato soup. He adds chopped celery too, but we don't have any.

I hear Mom's feet on the stairs. I don't want to get in trouble again for cooking, so I quickly turn the burner off and position myself in front of the pot to block it from view, in case she's just walking in to fill up her coffee mug.

"I thought I heard someone down here, but I wasn't sure if it was you or your sister," Mom says, lingering in the doorway. She has a white business envelope in one hand, and she's tapping it against her other palm.

We haven't made up yet from yesterday, and since Allie wasn't around in the evening, we didn't even watch TV together after dinner. Mom went up to her room to work, and I watched a documentary about a recently discovered tomb in Egypt.

"What's in the envelope?" I ask.

"Nothing," she says, immediately putting it behind her back.

I step toward her, forgetting about hiding the pot on the stove, and hold my hand out. "It's obviously *something*. Can I see it?"

Mom holds tight to the envelope. She doesn't offer it to me.

"Mom?"

She sighs heavily. "It's about school. You were wait-listed at the magnet."

"Wait-listed?" I snatch the envelope from her, which feels worn and slightly crumpled, as if it's been held and read more than once.

I slide two fingers in the top and pull out the papers. The top page is a letter. It reads:

To the parents of Virginia Pierce:

Thank you for your interest in the Montgomery County Public Schools magnet program. Your daughter's test scores have qualified her for a spot at Reddington Math & Science School. However, we regret to inform you that enrollment is already at capacity, and we are unable to register your daughter for the upcoming academic year.

She has been placed on the wait list for her grade level, and we will inform you promptly if a spot becomes available.

In the meantime, please find enclosed some after-school enrichment programs offered for gifted children.

The kitchen is absolutely silent. I feel like the world is spinning and spinning around me, like I'm standing on the equator and can actually feel the earth's rotation.

"I didn't get in," I whisper.

Mom pastes on a fake smile and says, "You *did* get in, you're just on the wait list. I'm sure they'll have room at some point."

"When? A *year* from now? What happens until then?"

I start panicking, trying to imagine what it'll be like to be back in regular school. Classrooms full of obnoxious Joey Bingles. Or worse.

Mom fills a glass of water at the sink and hands it to me. "Ginny, I know this is a shock."

I accept the glass but end up gulping too fast. I cough the water out and wipe my mouth with the back of my arm.

"I know it probably feels like the end of the world right now," Mom says. "But it's not. And at least you and Allie will be at the same school again."

Is she kidding? Does Mom really have no idea what's going on with me and Allie?

I jam the papers back into the envelope and don't respond. As soon as Mom leaves, I'm going to rip them into a thousand pieces and flush them down the toilet. I wish I could throw them into the Gulf of Corryvreckan, off the coast of Scotland, which is one of the largest permanent whirlpools in the world. Maybe I could throw myself in too.

"You and Allie can ride the bus together," Mom continues. "You'll both know someone on the very first day."

Every single word she's saying is *making this worse.* Doesn't she know that?

"Allie won't *want* me on the bus with her!" I burst out. "Or in the same *building.*"

Saying it makes me realize how much it hurts that my sister doesn't want me anywhere near her social circle. I knew it in my gut already, but it's different when you say it out loud.

Something changes on Mom's face. There's a flicker of understanding. She nods slowly and says, "I'm sure it feels like that sometimes. But it's not true."

Of course it's true—Mom just won't admit it. She's being as phony as Dad's emails. Can't anyone tell the truth around here?

"The wait list will work out, Ginny," she drones on. "There are always families who move at the last minute or switch their kids to private school, and then spots open up. I think if we're patient, you'll be at the magnet soon."

I hold up a hand. "Please stop. Be honest with me for once. This is bad news—admit it."

Mom sighs. "It's not ideal, Ginny. But we'll make it work, like we make everything else around here work."

That's a laugh. As far as I'm concerned, nothing around here is working.

Dad wouldn't just say *it's not ideal* and make me sit around for a year, hoping to get in. But Dad isn't here to fix this for me—I have to fix it for myself.

"I need to go to that school," I say. "I'm going to call them myself tomorrow and explain why."

Mom's turned the burner back on under the soup, and she's standing there stirring it, her back to me. After a minute, she says, "I think that's a great idea, Ginny, and I'm proud of you for advocating for yourself. But I want to make sure you understand that sometimes things don't work out the way we want them to. We have to do the best we can with what we get."

She's making me feel like I'm a toddler upset about getting the wrong doll for my birthday. This is my *school*—my entire academic life.

"I understand perfectly," I tell her.

"Good," Mom says. "And there's one more thing...."

I brace myself. What more could there be?

"I think you've been spending too much time alone. Starting tomorrow, you're going back to that jewelry camp for the rest of the session."

I can't believe what I'm hearing. First I don't get into the magnet school and now *I'm being sent to jewelry prison*?

"Mom, *no*! I'm not going back there! No one talked about anything except bead patterns!"

Mom takes the pot off the stove and pours the soup into two bowls. She brings them over to the table and sets one in front of me.

"I know this probably seems harsh to you, but I've given it a lot of thought. Sometimes you don't give things a chance. And with this school news, well, the jewelry camp might be a helpful step in getting you acclimated."

"You don't get it," I yell, jumping up and shoving my chair into the table so hard that soup sloshes out of the bowls. "YOU DON'T GET ME AT ALL!"

My feet pound up the stairs to my room, grateful at least that Allie's door is still closed. Because as soon as she finds out I didn't get into the STEM magnet, things will be even worse. She'll probably tell everyone on the street so they can have a good laugh at me.

Before he left, Dad promised me I'd get in. He said it would be no problem that my application was two months late. He said this was one of those perks of being a military kid that's supposed to make up for the bad stuff, like having to move constantly and having one of your parents ship off every few years to the other side of the world.

I thought Dad was my hero. But he lied to me, and now he's not even here to help me through this.

I can't go back to a regular school. Once classes start and I'm answering every question and getting straight As, no one will want to hang out with me. No one will even talk to me.

Alone in my room, I grab the map I made of the Atlantic Ocean floor and rip it in half. Then I pick up my Serengeti map, still unfinished, and rip that too.

Ripping poster board is hard but satisfying.

I look at my globe, perched proudly on my desk, taunting me with an entire world of places I'd rather be than here in Silver Spring.

I shove my window open, pick up the globe, and hurl it outside. It lands in the purple butterfly bush with a satisfying thud.

I slide my window shut and climb onto my bed, pulling the covers over my head. Tears are falling fast and hot now, and I cry into the pillow so Allie won't hear me.

I'm angry at my mom for making me go back to camp, but I'm even more angry with Dad.

None of this would have happened if he hadn't deployed.

Fact: In the winter of 1811–12, a series of very strong earthquakes and their aftershocks made the Mississippi River appear to flow backward. Scientists later determined that the earthquakes had magnitudes of 7.3 to 7.5 and caused waves that moved upstream.

I lay awake for hours last night, thinking about my situation.

In the wild, if animals can't adapt to their environment, they die. In southern Africa, the Cape ground squirrel has evolved and learned to use its own tail as a parasol to shade it from the hot sun.

Can I evolve too? And if so, do I want to?

As I'm putting my lunch in my backpack and filling my water bottle for camp, Allie sits silently, eating her breakfast. Even though she doesn't know about my school letter yet, she knows Mom is sending me back to jewelry camp.

I expect her to gloat, or at least look superior, about how she gets to enjoy a day of nonstop games and fun in the neighborhood without me around to ruin her good time. Instead, she looks sulky.

"What's up with you?"

"Nothing," she mutters.

"Still mad at me about the panda thing?"

She glances up, a look of exasperation on her face. "Not everything is about *you*, Ginny."

Mom comes flying down the stairs, still in her pajamas, and stops short when she sees me standing with my backpack.

"You're ready?" she asks, surprised. "That's great! Let's go. I've got to be back here for a call in forty minutes. Allie, are you fine with—"

"Don't worry about me," Allie snaps.

Mom opens and closes her mouth several times, as if considering whether to reply. Then she picks up her keys and heads to the garage.

I look at Allie, wondering what could be going on. She and Mom hardly ever fight. Why is Allie being so rude? And why didn't Mom yell at her for it?

The drive to camp is tense and silent. When we arrive at the drop-off spot, I say, "Pickup is at three o'clock. Please don't be late."

"I won't," she promises. "You can do this, Ginny. You're tougher than you think."

I picture myself in my pith helmet and safari clothes, trekking up to Machu Picchu with Dad in a few years. I suppose I'll have to be pretty tough for that. This is just jewelry camp, after all. How bad can it be?

As soon as I walk through the door of room 213, everyone stops what they're doing and stares at me. One girl's mouth actually drops open. I feel my face instantly turn red, certain I'm covered in green slime or scales or I've grown a Cape ground squirrel tail without realizing it.

"You came back," Manda says, visibly surprised. "We thought you'd quit!"

Other kids chime in with various questions. "Yeah, what happened?" "Where were you?"

I hadn't bothered to come up with a reason why I've missed nearly half the camp. I didn't think anyone would notice. I guess I should have known that kids who can memorize the complicated Russian chevron pattern are going to notice when one kid in a room of twenty is missing. Especially if that kid wore a weird hat the first day.

My instincts tell me to lie.

"Nothing happened," I say, wracking my brain for an excuse. "My grandparents came for a surprise visit."

Smiles break out all over the classroom, and Manda gives me a thumbs-up. A girl with orangey-red hair says, "Oh good! We thought it was us."

A few girls laugh. Overall, everyone seems relieved, almost as if they'd been taking it personally that I hadn't returned.

I'm baffled. Is it possible these girls thought I didn't like *them*? I thought they didn't like *me*.

Manda waves me over to an empty seat by Supriya. "You missed a lot," she says, "but Supriya will help you catch up. Today we're going to try some Dutch spirals. If you have questions, ask right away, otherwise you'll get stuck. It's like knitting, right? You don't want to unravel the whole row because of one bad stitch."

Again, laughter from the group. Everyone seems more chatty and relaxed than they did on the first day.

I sit down beside Supriya and whisper, "Did I really miss a lot?"

"Yeah," she says. "I'm glad you came back, though. No one's told me a single thing about continental drift since you left."

I feel my heart expand in my chest. "You remember me telling you about continental drift?"

"Of course I remember! It's not something I talk about every day, you know."

I nod as if I agree, but personally, I would love to talk about it every day.

"Please don't tell anyone my grandparents weren't really visiting," I say. "I'm surprised anyone even noticed I was gone."

"I won't tell. But they definitely noticed—and they wanted to make sure you didn't leave because you hate crafting, even though you told me you do." She smiles at me conspiratorially.

"Why would they care if I hate it?"

"Because when you love something enough to spend three weeks at camp doing it, you want to meet other people who love it too."

What she's saying is so obvious, and yet it's like the difference between theoretically knowing that the earth is round, and actually seeing its curvature when you stare out at the horizon over the ocean. I see it now. To me, making bracelets is frustrating. But to them, it probably feels creative and challenging.

I could have been nicer about it. I could have made it less obvious I wasn't interested in being here.

Honestly, I'm *still* not interested in being here. But I guess that's no reason to ruin it for everyone else.

Manda gives us printouts of the Dutch spiral pattern to follow, and I vow to try my best today.

Unfortunately, even my best isn't good enough, because I mess up over and over again. I know it sounds easy to follow a pattern, but for this one you have to *stitch* the beads around each other to hold the spiral shape, and you have to line them all up correctly each time. And if you let your mind wander and start thinking about the melting polar ice caps, you end up with your rows all sewn together and your pattern messed up.

Supriya comes to the rescue a few times, but I stop asking her when I realize I'm taking up all the time she should be working on her own piece. Feeling mildly humiliated, I raise my hand and wait for Manda to come to my desk.

I'm not used to being bad at something. I'm not used to having to ask for help or having something explained to me. It's embarrassing.

Manda picks up my work, scrunching her nose in a way that tells me it's really off. She starts removing beads, explaining as she goes that the Dutch spiral is basically just a "peyote stitch spine with a beaded swag."

I pay attention while she talks, but I know once I start doing it myself, my mind will wander, and I'll mess up again. I just can't get my brain to focus on something that doesn't interest me very much.

"Manda?" I say, looking back and forth between her and my bracelet. "I'm having a hard time with this pattern. Is it okay if I make something else?"

Manda nods, looking surprisingly sympathetic. "Sure. Look in the supply bins. Whatever we have, you can use. Make something *you* like."

She pats my shoulder and moves on to help someone else. Feeling like the world's biggest loser, I get up and go to the front of the room to look through the bins. There are so many different kinds of beads and floss. I see a container of beads with numbers on them and get an idea.

I start working on a new bracelet, making it more complicated than just a single one-strander but easier than the advanced patterns the class is working on. I get stuck a few times, and somehow, without me even saying anything, Supriya knows and puts her work down to help me.

She never acts like she knows more than I do. She just calmly picks up my work, shows me where I went off the path, and points me back on.

I want to ask her if the water park was fun, and if she likes Allie more than me now. But what if the answer is yes?

After the second or third time she helps me, I whisper, "Supriya, am I too nerdy to hang out with?"

Supriya's eyebrows shoot up in surprise. She shakes her head. "No way, Ginny. You know about things and places I've never even heard of—and I'm older than you! I'd say you're...*unique*."

Unique. There are a lot of unique things in the world, like Devils Tower in Wyoming, which is a massive formation made of a rare igneous rock rising up from the grasslands. Geologists have been studying it for over a century and still don't agree on how it was created.

They do agree that it's a wonder.

I look at Supriya, working diligently on her bracelet. She's easy to talk to, like Dad. I want to tell her a fact so badly that I have that holding-a-sneeze feeling. I want to tell her the moon is shriveling up like a grape, and that it's causing moonquakes, which are like earthquakes but on the moon.

But this is jewelry camp, and today I'm a Cape ground squirrel. So I hold in my fact sneeze and ask her something Allie would approve of. I say, "What grade are you in, and what's your school like?"

"I'm going into eighth grade, but I don't go to Greenwood Middle like everyone else on the block. I go to a STEM magnet school—Reddington."

Supriya goes to Reddington?

I drop my bracelet and several of the number beads slip off and clatter onto the desk. Just when I thought things couldn't get worse, I find out the one person I've met here who isn't allergic to the words "continental drift" goes to the school I couldn't get into.

I scramble to pick up my beads and decide not to tell her my situation in case she tells Rihan who'll tell Allie.

"Reddington?" I repeat, as nonchalantly as possible. "What's it like?"

Supriya starts talking, describing the science labs and how she dissected a synthetic frog last year, how much time they have for independent project work, and suddenly the minutes are flying by.

"It sounds perfect," I say, unable to keep the envy out of my voice. Every single word is seared into my brain. Reddington is the school for me.

"Well, it's not *perfect*," she replies. "I mean, it's a good school, but the commute is long—I have to take two buses each way. And the kids that go there come from all over the county, so most of my friends don't live nearby. And sometimes the workload can be too much. I mean, it's just middle school, right?"

I digest this. I, personally, have always wished for more work at school. How else am I going to be prepared to make an important geographic discovery one day? But I suppose her other points are good.

"What's your favorite area of science?" I ask. "I mean, why'd you end up going to a STEM school?"

"I'm really into biology and studying nature and patterns. That's why I like beading and friendship bracelets. Also, because my mom told me I had to find a non-science 'creative outlet' to get me off my computer, so this is what I chose."

Her mother sounds a lot like mine.

The girl next to me asks to borrow my scissors, and I hand them to her. She smiles at me when she hands them back.

Her smile is warm and friendly. Before I know what I'm doing, I'm complimenting her project. She's managed to replicate the Dutch spiral pattern flawlessly.

"Oh, thanks!" she says, pleased. "It's one of my favorite patterns we've done. What about you, Marissa?" she says, nudging the girl beside her. "What's your favorite thing we've done here so far?"

The two girls start talking about a pattern they worked on last week, and Supriya joins in. I'm disappointed our chat about Reddington is over. I wanted to hear more details so I can wallow over them later. Or use them when I call the school board—maybe I can explain that I know someone there and how perfect it is for me.

But for the rest of today, I make myself listen to the girls' conversation, and it isn't so terrible. When Marissa asks me where I go to school, I change the subject slightly by telling them that I've just moved to Maryland and that I've lived in five different states. They find that interesting and ask me questions about my favorite place I've lived.

While we talk and they perfect their Dutch spirals, I keep working on my project. It's a geography bracelet with the numbered beads showing the latitude and longitude of the Bagram Airfield. They're the closest coordinates I have to where Dad is right now.

When it's done, I tie it on and rub my finger up and down the coordinates. It looks nothing like the elaborate projects everyone else has been working on, but I don't care.

My bracelet is unique, like me.

21,

Fact: Oymyakon, Russia, is considered the world's coldest permanently inhabited town, with its lowest officially recorded temperature being minus 96.16 degrees Fahrenheit. That's colder than the average temperature on Mars, which is 81 below zero.

When I get home from camp, I run straight to my room to look up the Montgomery County School Board's number so I can call and try to get myself into Reddington.

But when I turn on the tablet, I see I have three missed calls from Dad and a one-line email asking me to call him back.

He finally called and I missed it because of stupid jewelry camp!?

I immediately try calling him. I try several times but only get his voice mail. I leave him a message that I'm home now and to call me again. Then I look up the school board number and dial it. I get a recorded message that their summer hours are 9:00 AM to 3:30 PM, which means I can't call them while camp is going on.

I leave them a voice mail explaining my situation and asking if there's a day I can call them back later than 3:30.

Frustrated, I carry the tablet downstairs with me to find Mom and tell her Dad called.

She's in the kitchen starting dinner. I feel a surge of joy when I see her holding a packet of fajita mix. As upset as I am about missing Dad's calls and the revelation that Supriya goes to Reddington, at least it's fajita night. Warm fajitas smothered in sour cream is my favorite dinner.

"We're out of sour cream," Mom announces before I can say anything. "And, *yes,* I'm aware that no one has clean underwear. I'll try to do the laundry tonight."

I clutch the tablet to my chest and freeze. I thought *I* was the one having a bad day. What happened to super-human Military Mom? For once, I wish Allie were here to make a joke and cut the tension in the room.

"It's okay, Mom," I say.

I lean against the counter, watching as she assembles the ingredients, knives, and cutting board. It doesn't seem like she wants to talk, but I have to ask about Dad.

"Did you talk to Dad today? He called while I was at camp and I just tried to call him back, but he didn't answer."

"Yes, I did talk to him," she says, her shoulders relaxing slightly. "Although only for a minute. Their Wi-Fi has been down, but it's back up now, so I'm sure he'll try you again as soon as he has a minute."

So the Wi-Fi *has* been the problem. Why does everyone think Wi-Fi makes it easier to connect? Dad says in the old days of deployments, families got two twenty-minute calls per week over a DSN (Defense Switched Network) line with their loved one. That at least sounds reliable.

"Did you tell him about Reddington?" I ask.

Mom turns away to grab another knife. "I told him about you getting wait-listed," she says. "And he was very upset, even though we knew it was a long shot, since we applied so late."

A long shot? No one told me it was a long shot. And if it was, then why did Dad practically promise me he'd take care of it?

"Maybe you guys should have told me that, instead of telling me I'd get in."

I pause, waiting to see how Mom reacts. She doesn't.

I go on. "Rihan's sister, who's at my jewelry camp, goes there. She loves it. Says it's amazing. *That's* where I should be going to school."

"You said you were going to try calling them," Mom says.

"I did. They close at 3:30 PM in the summer. So I won't be able to talk to them until after next week if you keep making me go to jewelry camp."

Mom takes a deep breath. "Fine. I will call them tomorrow, Ginny. But I don't know that it'll change anything."

Feeling somewhat mollified, I watch Mom rinse a wrinkled red pepper under the faucet and place it on the cutting board.

"What else did Dad say?" I ask. "What's it like at the CSH? How come we still don't know anything about what he's doing?"

"We know exactly what he's doing. He works long hours. He sleeps. He eats. He exercises. That's about it."

She starts chopping the pepper vigorously, bringing the knife down hard on the wooden cutting board.

Chop. CHOP. CHOP.

"I need to hear it from him myself," I say. "I can hardly sleep some nights, worrying about him and wondering if he's okay. I've been reading the headlines every day—"

"That's the worst thing you can do," Mom cuts in. "Believe me. Better to find a really good book. Organize your room. Bake something."

"I can't—you won't let me use the oven."

Mom narrows her eyes at me. "That doesn't seem to be stopping you, though, does it?"

I shake my head. "I guess not."

"Listen, we just have to trust that things are fine. Your dad is with the best people, and they're being as safe as possible."

As usual, her words sound rehearsed. The pile of pepper slices grows. I touch her elbow to get her to stop chopping. "Mom—please stop sounding like an army brochure and talk to me."

Mom puts the knife down and sighs. She looks at me, and I'm surprised by how hollow her eyes are. "I know you're having a terrible time right now, Ginny. But for me, the months *before* your dad deploys are the hardest. Because I'm dreading it so much. And your dad and I fight more because we're both unhappy about him leaving. So when he finally deploys, it's almost a relief.

Because I know that things will be calm. And I can start counting the days until he's home. There's plenty to do with my work, and I have you and Allie."

"But you don't have *Dad*!"

She nods. "I know. And I'll tell you something—missing him myself isn't nearly as hard as watching you miss him."

Her eyes tear up. It's such a rare sight that I hop up from the stool and throw my arms around her. She hugs me back hard, much harder than she usually does. I feel her take a raggedy breath, then a few slow, deep ones.

Feeling bold, because we can't see each other's faces, I ask, "Were you always this tough, Mom? Or did becoming a military wife make you like this?"

Mom releases me, wiping at one of her eyes with the back of her hand. "Oh, I'm not so tough, kiddo."

I think she is. She's the perfect military wife. I, on the other hand, am the total opposite of what military kids are supposed to be: resilient and flexible, with great social skills.

"You have to learn to take things one day at a time," Mom says, as she carries the cut veggies to the stove. "Some days, one minute at a time. That's why I sent you back to jewelry camp even though I know it isn't your thing—I thought it might help the minutes go by faster."

She's right. Camp did make the day go faster, but I also missed Dad's call. But what if he *hadn't* called me? What if he doesn't call me back again for several days? I can't sit by the tablet all day.

Mom hands me the tongs. "How about for right now, you just help me make the fajitas?"

I nod. Maybe it's not a bad idea to try this one-minute-at-a-time stuff.

Mom claps. "Okay, then. Start by adding some oil to the frying pan—just a tablespoon or two. Let it heat through, then toss in the chicken. Move it around a bit and make sure to turn each piece over a few times."

I click the tongs together and get to work. I methodically turn over each piece of chicken every minute. The kitchen starts to smell good.

"Watch it," Mom warns. "Don't let them burn."

She begins filling bowls with toppings—shredded cheese, green onions. All four of us like green onions, so we always have them for taco night and fajita night. Dad sometimes sneaks a few into a napkin and hides it on his chair before dinner starts to make sure he gets enough.

I picture Dad sitting at the table at our old house, holding his napkin and laughing about his onion trick.

My heart clenches. Missing him is physically painful.

One minute at a time. I try desperately to think of something to distract myself.

"Mom, did you know that in Japan, if you stick your chopsticks upright in your rice bowl, it offends people? Do you want to know why?"

"Um, sure," she says, unconvincingly.

"Never mind. I think the chicken's cooked. I'll set the table."

"I'm sorry. Please—tell me. Why does putting chopsticks like that offend people?"

Now I don't even want to tell her, but I have to since she feels bad. "Because during funerals they put a bowl of rice by the dead person's coffin, with the chopsticks upright to symbolize that the person has died. So it reminds people of funerals, and it's considered bad luck."

Mom's stoic face cracks a smile. Then she can't stop herself, and she breaks out into a full-blown laugh. "Where did you come from, Ginny? And what would we do without you?"

I avoid her eyes. "I think Allie could do without me just fine."

"No, she couldn't," she says firmly. "She may not know that at the moment because she's an almost-teenaged girl, but *I* know it. And remember, she's having a hard time too. You aren't the only one who misses Dad. Sometimes you like to think Dad is all yours."

I know Allie misses Dad, but it's different. I *need* him.

Mom studies me. "I'm going to tell you something serious because I think it'll help you."

I nod, my muscles tensing up. "Something about Dad?"

"No. About your sister." Mom transfers the cooked chicken to a plate and puts the peppers and onions in the pan to sauté. "She got her new school schedule, and she was placed in the section for kids who are approaching grade level."

"You mean she won't be in seventh grade?"

"No, she's in seventh grade. But this school system has tracking. And based on her standardized test scores, she's in the group that has some catching up to do. She won't be able to take a foreign language this year, and she's disappointed about that."

"Really? I've never heard Allie say she cares about studying a language."

Mom cocks her head and looks at me. "It isn't always easy for her to be your sister."

I suppose it is pretty hard to have a younger sister who learned to read before you did. But there's so much that's easy for Allie. Like sports and friendships and just life in general.

She may not be able to take a foreign language, but she'll probably make ten new friends at Greenwood the very first week and be elected class vice president. Meanwhile, I'll answer too many questions correctly and be relegated to social Siberia, which is an area of Russia so cold and remote that historically it's been used as a place to exile and imprison people.

The veggies are starting to smell a little burnt, so Mom scoops up the pan to move it off the burner. "Go call your sister in, please."

"Does she know about me being wait-listed?"

Mom turns away as she distributes the chicken. "No, she doesn't. But you should probably mention it soon, since you'll be going to Greenwood with her and some of the kids on the street."

I haven't really thought about the fact that Rihan and Kayla will be at Greenwood too. Will I have classes with them? Will they talk to me?

I call Allie in by ringing the schoolhouse bell. When she bursts into the house, her face is pink and shining from running around. There's no sign of the sulky Allie I saw at breakfast, the one Mom says is upset about school. She monopolizes dinner by staging an elaborate retelling of some game she and Rihan played with the Stein brothers all afternoon. I focus on my fajitas and keep my mouth shut.

After dinner, Mom heads back upstairs to work, and I find Allie flopped on the couch with the remote. I wonder if she's thinking and worrying about school.

"I saw this documentary the other night about a newly discovered tomb in Egypt," I tell her, perching on the edge of Dad's recliner. "It was really interesting and showed how archaeologists excavate the artifacts and clean them, and how they translate the writing they find."

"Mmm," Allie says, flipping through channels until she finds an old rom-com.

"I don't mind watching it again if you want to see it."

"No, thanks."

"It would probably be really helpful for seventh-grade history," I add. "You know, if you wanted to get a head start or something."

Allie looks at me, suspicious. "Why would I want to do that?"

"I don't know. No reason."

If she'd let me, I could get her into the grade-level group in no time.

"I. Want. To. Watch. A. Movie," she says, enunciating each word clearly. "So why don't you go upstairs and make a map or something."

I blink. It's gotten so hard to even talk to her. "I'm just trying to help."

"Help with *what*?" she asks.

"Nothing," I say, frustrated. Why can't Allie and I just be honest with each other? I could tell her about my letter and she could tell me about hers. "I only meant it would be fun to watch it together."

"It wouldn't be fun for me. Can you please leave me alone?"

I nod, feeling deflated. I wish we could talk about Dad or school or *something*. But it's like we're from two different planets.

Fact: The Eiffel Tower can grow several inches taller in warm weather. The hot sun beating down on the iron tower makes the metal expand, causing the whole structure to grow. This growth is temporary, and in cold weather the tower contracts.

I return to jewelry camp with a better attitude. It's not my favorite place to be, but it's a routine. I look at it as a challenge—what simple things can I come up with to make jewelry camp a little better each day?

First, I make sure to sit next to Supriya. She's by far my favorite person there, and she doesn't care when I talk about things other than the project we're working on. I tell her about the Egyptian tomb documentary, and she promises to watch it.

Second, I accept that we're going to spend the entire day sitting and crafting and that my mind will wander. I bring a pencil and a notepad so I can doodle maps when I need a break. I also challenge myself to come up with some riddles that I can send to Dad later.

Third, I adjust my expectations of what I'm able to create and how it compares to what the other girls in the group create. If a pattern is too hard, I tweak it and make it my own.

All this has helped make the quiet days at camp feel almost pleasant. It's certainly preferable to being at home, where Allie is still half-ignoring me and spends all her time outside with Rihan, and Mom is laser focused on her work project.

Dad hasn't called again, although I got another email from him that said: *Send me more updates! Can't wait to talk to you!*

Without Dad to balance us out, the level of tension in our house seems to be growing worse and worse. We're like an overstretched rubber band, ready to snap.

On Friday morning, we start on yet another complicated friendship bracelet pattern—this time weaving a butterfly repeat design with the threads. I'm trying hard, but it's tedious, and I'm dying to talk about something. I've already sketched out a map of Brazil on my notepad, which is the most biodiverse country on the planet and includes approximately 60 percent of the Amazon rain forest.

Two other girls, Miri and Gretchen, sit with their chairs turned toward me and Supriya. They seem friendly. Mostly they talk about our jewelry projects or movies or their summer vacation plans. I manage to stay part of the conversation, just by nodding and agreeing with things, but since today is the last day of camp, I decide to take a risk.

I clear my throat, which feels thick and sludgy from pretend-talking instead of actual talking. Unfortunately, I clear it too hard, and end up having to do it a second time, just to soothe it from the first. I sound like I have tuberculosis.

I take a deep breath and go for it. "If you could spend the day with anyone in the world, who would it be?"

Miri and Gretchen exchange a sideways glance but don't reply. Thankfully, Supriya jumps in.

"*Anyone?*" she asks. "Dead or alive?"

I nod.

"Well, that's easy," she replies. "Jane Goodall. She discovered that chimpanzees make tools, hunt and eat meat, and have social structures similar to humans. She's my hero."

"Good choice," I say, feeling yet another stab of disappointment that I won't be going to school with her. "Gretchen?"

Gretchen blushes and shifts in her seat. "I don't know. Ummm...Riley Knowlton? You know, from that movie *No Boundaries for Us*? He's so cute."

Miri enthusiastically nods her agreement, and I smile back, pretending to know who this actor is. He's no Jane Goodall, that's for sure.

"What about you, Miri?" Supriya asks.

Miri looks up and purses her lips, as if thinking hard. "I don't know. Maybe my grandma? Because she died when I was little and I didn't get to know her very well."

"I love that answer," I say, meaning it. It's not quite the point of the question but it does tell me something about Miri—she loves her family.

Miri looks pleased with my reaction. "What about you, Ginny?" she asks. "Who would you like to spend a day with?"

"Me? Definitely Marie Tharp. She was one of the four greatest cartographers of the twentieth century and helped prove the theory of plate tectonics. She's *my* hero."

Miri and Gretchen both stare at me, mouths hanging open.

Oh well. There goes that.

Then Supriya picks up her bracelet and asks, "Does anyone know how much time we have for these? I want to add another color. Or maybe two. What do you think?"

She holds up two possible extra thread color choices, and Miri and Gretchen offer their opinions. A minute later, when the other girls are working intently on their projects again, Supriya looks over at me with a smile and a knowing look.

She asked that question for *me*. She distracted them for me.

A bunch of gears in my head start turning and clicking. I remember how yesterday, Gretchen started to make a not-nice comment about another girl in the class, and Supriya immediately changed the subject by mentioning that she really needed a new bathing suit.

Supriya is a nice person. And a smart person. And, most importantly, she seems to like me pretty well.

I thought things couldn't be worse. But they could. They definitely could.

After lunch, Manda makes an announcement.

"You've all done *so* well these past three weeks that I want us to have a jewelry showcase! So choose your favorite piece that you've made, the one you feel represents *you* the most. Then during our last half hour of camp today, I'd like each of you to come up to the front of the room and show it off. Tell us why you picked it and what you liked best about making it. Okay?"

A *showcase?*

Total panic. I look at my pieces—which are few compared to everyone else. I missed nearly half of camp, and everything takes me so long to make. I have my geography bracelet, which is simple and not visually impressive. Yesterday and today, I tried to complete the Russian chevron bracelet pattern we got on the first day, to see if I could do it. I could not.

Then there's my failed Dutch spiral. And today's butterfly pattern. I would like to say it's as beautiful as Saint Basil's Cathedral in Moscow, which has colorful onion domes of different heights and resembles the flames of a bonfire, but it's not. I got about 70 percent of the pattern correct, which is less than I've ever scored on any test or project in my life. I don't want to get up and present it to a room full of girls who made multiple complicated 3D patterns.

"Do you think I could skip presenting?" I whisper to Supriya, who has a gorgeous peyote stitch project to show, as well as several other pieces that look great.

"Why?"

"This is why." I point to my bumpy, messy Russian chevron.

"Your bracelet is fine. Anyway, who cares?"

Who cares? *I* do. I care that these other girls are so much better at something than I am. Don't I?

I fiddle with my 70-percent-correct bracelet. My work, no matter the type of work, has always been excellent. I can't go up there with this thing.

"I can't do this," I say.

"You're overthinking it," Supriya replies. "Just talk about how this was the first time you'd ever tried this and how much you learned. Some of these girls come every year."

That makes me feel better. No wonder they're so good at it.

During the showcase, Supriya gets called up first. She shows her peyote stitch piece, and listening to her talk makes me feel strangely sad.

Now that I've gotten to know her, I really want her to be my friend. And once this camp is over, and she's back at home all day, she'll probably end up hanging out with Allie and Rihan.

One by one, the other girls present their impressive projects. I get called last.

Supriya nods at me encouragingly, and I grab my butterfly bracelet and stand up.

But then I put it back down. Manda said to pick the piece that best represents me. Not the one that was the hardest or looks the most impressive. Just the one that's the most *me*.

So I march to the front of the classroom, unclasping the only bracelet I've ever worn in my life from my left wrist. My geography bracelet.

I hold it up. "I made this the other day. It's not complicated, and there's no pattern, but the numbers are the coordinates to the Bagram Airfield in Afghanistan. My dad is a doctor in the Army Medical Corps, and he's deployed there until December. I made this bracelet because..." I pause, trying to articulate why I made the bracelet.

So that I could think of him whenever I look at it? To show that even though he's *there*, he's *here* with me too?

Those reasons aren't really why I made it. Why not just tell the truth?

"I actually made it for him," I say. "Because it's a friendship bracelet, and my dad is my best friend. We move a lot, and sometimes it's hard for me to make friends."

I stop talking then. The girls in the classroom are all staring at me, unsure how to respond.

But Supriya is smiling supportively, and she's the one I care about most.

Manda says, "Thanks for sharing that, Ginny. I'm glad the art we've created here has been meaningful for you."

The art we've created here. I didn't think of this as art— just crafts. But it's so much more than that to these girls, just the way maps are so much more than maps to me. They're not only an intellectual outlet for me, they're my creative outlet too.

Maybe I won't ever have a ton of friends like Allie does or meet many kids who are like me. But I can still *be* me.

I can still follow my true north.

"Oh, and one final thing," I announce. "Did you know that the ears of African elephants are large and shaped like the continent of Africa, while the ears of Asian elephants are smaller and shaped more like India? It makes them really easy to tell apart."

I grab a piece of chalk and draw the shapes of Africa and India on the board, to illustrate my point.

When I turn back around, the group is speechless.

I take a small bow, then return to my seat, feeling like I'm about to sob, but also like I might be okay.

Fact: 3,160 tons of water flow over Niagara Falls every single second. In 1901, a sixty-three-year-old woman became the first person to go over the falls in a barrel and survive.

On Sunday morning, I'm reading on the front porch when Mom yells, "Allie! Ginny! Come here! *Now!*"

Panicked, I drop my book and run into the house. Mom's in the kitchen, sitting at the table with her laptop. Her hand is pressed to her mouth, and there are tears in her eyes. Allie thunders down the stairs and nearly knocks me over as she rushes into the room behind me.

"What's wrong?" she yells.

"Nothing!" Mom says, still teary. "Dad's on video-chat. Come say hi."

We scramble around the kitchen table to Mom's side, and there he is—Dad. And yet it *isn't* Dad. His face is sunburned, and he's grown a mustache. He's not wearing his glasses.

But he's okay. *He's okay.*

I feel dizzy with relief. I plant my hands on the table to steady myself as Allie shoves in next to me. Mom moves over so we can see Dad better and sits there clutching her coffee mug and blinking rapidly.

"Dad!" Allie shouts. "How are you?"

"Allie! Ginny!" Dad's face breaks into a huge smile, and he holds his arms out wide as if to pull us both into a hug. "It's so good to see your faces. I'm sorry I haven't been calling—we had an incident when I first arrived, and the Wi-Fi has been in and out ever since. They finally fixed it properly this morning."

"What kind of incident?" I ask. "A truck bomb?"

Beside me, Allie sucks in a breath.

"It's nothing to worry about," Dad says, a little too casually. "What have you girls been doing? I want to hear everything."

He's changing the subject. I want to call him on it but I've been storing up so many things to tell him that I'm full to bursting. The problem is, I don't know where to start.

"Well, there's this—" I begin, but Allie cuts me off.

"The kids here are really nice," she says. "I've made a bunch of friends. And I'm playing basketball every day, so I'll be ready for fall tryouts, and there's a creek nearby that we can ride our bikes to. Oh, and I went to a water park and to the pool with a neighbor a few times."

"That's great, Allie," Dad says, visibly relieved. "Mom and I were hoping you'd like the new neighborhood. How about you, Ginny?"

I open my mouth, but then close it again. I can't follow Allie's amazing updates with "I survived jewelry camp" and "I've read a bunch of books."

Allie elbows me, urging me to speak. I know she'll start talking about herself again if I don't say something.

A voice on Dad's end calls out, and Dad waves his hand at the person and mumbles something like *Be there soon.*

"You don't have to hang up, do you?" I ask. "It's only been two minutes!"

"No, not yet," he says. "But I don't have a lot of time. Tell me about you, Ginny."

I can't tell him how miserable and lonely the last few weeks have been. Not like this—not in front of Mom and Allie.

Instead, I say, "Why do you have that mustache?"

Dad touches it tentatively. "You don't like it? All the guys here are growing them. It's a contest."

"You don't look like yourself."

"I like it," Allie chimes in. I elbow her and Mom hisses "Stop!" at us under her breath.

Dad shrugs. "Well, I don't think I'm winning the contest anyway, so it might have to go." The expression on his face changes then, darkening, like a cloud passing overhead in the sky.

"Listen," he says. "I need to tell you guys something."

I feel Mom tense up beside me. "What is it, John?"

"The doctor I was supposed to split this deployment with is still having health issues and won't be able to take over for me in December," he says. "The good news is they've found someone to take his place. But the bad news is that he won't arrive until March. So it looks like I'm here until then."

March. MARCH?

That's *nine months* he'll be gone! He'll miss Christmas with us and most of the school year. So many things have happened already in the five weeks since he left—I could be a completely different person by the time he comes home. So could he.

I want to pick up the laptop and hurl it at the wall, but the "suggested guidelines" for phone calls from the military families guide flashes through my mind.

Only tell your deployed family member positive things.

Don't dwell on the negative.

Don't bring up "touchy issues" that can't be resolved in a phone call.

It does not advise throwing laptops.

"John, I really wish you would have told me first," Mom says, her voice wobbling. I turn to look at her and am surprised to see tears on her cheeks.

"I tried to, Liz, but you yelled for the kids before I could get to—"

Mom sniffs and wipes at her nose. She tries to put her Military Mom mask back on but it's too late. I've seen how she really feels, and if Mom thinks something is going to be hard, then it's really, *really* going to be hard.

"You have to come home in December," I plead. "You just have to. Please, Dad! *Please.*"

"Stop, Ginny!" Allie says angrily. "He *can't.*"

"I would if I could," Dad says. "But it's just three extra months. And everything is going pretty well there, right?"

"For Allie, yes. Not for *me!*" I start crying. More like sobbing. Mom puts her arm around me and leads me from the kitchen to the family room. I push her away, trying to get back to the laptop.

"Take a minute to get yourself together, Ginny," she says. "*Please.* Allie and I are digesting this too. Take some deep breaths, and let Allie talk to him alone for a minute. I'll call you in when it's your turn."

Mom's hands are shaking. I try to calm down while I wait, but as each precious minute passes, my anxiety increases, worried that Dad will have to hang up before I get my turn.

Finally, Allie and I swap places, and I'm alone in the kitchen with two-dimensional, mustached Dad. Allie turned her face away from me as I walked past her, but Dad's eyes are clearly red.

"I'm so sorry, Ginny," he says. "I wouldn't do this to you if I had a choice."

I nod. Logically, I know this isn't Dad's fault. I just can't believe how much harder his deployment is than I thought it would be.

"Let's not waste the only time we have to catch up," he says. "I know you have things to tell me."

"I did. Weeks ago. That's why I kept calling you and calling you!"

"There was no way for me to get through," he says patiently. "Believe me, there's nothing I'd rather do than talk to you." He forces a grin. "But you have me now! So tell me everything."

I've been waiting and wishing to talk to him, praying every second that he's okay. And now here he is, perfectly healthy, and somehow I have nothing to say. Video chat isn't like talking to him face-to-face. And now he's going to be gone even longer.

I'm angry at him. For being in the army and for leaving me.

Suddenly, the video pauses, and I panic, afraid I'm going to lose him. A few seconds later, he unfreezes.

But instead of feeling relieved, I'm even angrier. After weeks of the Wi-Fi being down, the connection *still* stinks? How does Dad think this is going to work?

"Mom told me about your school letter," he says. "And I'm so disappointed for you. I was sure it would work out."

"Why? We were two months late applying! You should have told me the truth."

He pauses. "Maybe I should have, but I thought we had a shot."

"A long shot."

He nods. "Yes, unfortunately. Mom called the school board, but it doesn't look good. She's also called the guidance counselor at Greenwood Middle, and she made sure they read your transcript and they're putting you in all the honors classes—"

"It's not just the school stuff, Dad," I cut in, the words tumbling out of me in a big, noisy rush. "Everything is terrible with you gone. I worry about you *all the time*. Allie and I fight constantly, and Mom is always working. And I miss talking to you. I miss asking you questions and telling you facts. You're the only person who likes—"

My voice breaks. I can't finish the sentence—*you're the only person who likes me just the way I am.*

I stare at my dad for a long, sad moment. "I need you here," I whisper.

"I know," he says. "But we can get through this. They say deployments make strong relationships stronger, and weak relationships fall apart. But *we* are the strong relationship, Ginny, okay?"

I don't answer. We were a strong relationship when

he left five weeks ago, but look how fast that's changed. Seven and a half more months is an eternity.

Mom barges in and jerks her head toward the front door, indicating I should go outside so they can talk alone.

My anger flashes again. "That's not fair! I only got a minute!"

"It's not fair," Mom agrees. "But Dad only has a few minutes today, and I get a turn too."

"We'll talk again in a few days," Dad promises. "Remember, the Wi-Fi is working here now. Let me talk to Mom alone, please."

I look from one parent to the other, both of them desperate to get me out of the way. I feel hot lava bubbling up inside me, ready to erupt.

"I hate you," I say to Mom. "You're always in a hurry or too busy to talk or you say generic things instead of being honest. You're supposed to take care of us while Dad's gone, but you just hide in your room!"

I turn to Dad on the screen, who looks stunned. "And I hate *you* for leaving me! Because of YOU we had to move to this awful town, by ourselves, while you're far away! I HATE YOU EVEN MORE!"

Before either of them can say anything, I knock over the kitchen chair beside me and run out of the room. I storm out onto the front porch, into a blast of humid air, tears pouring down my cheeks.

As the door slams shut, I hear Mom's voice crack as she says, "What are we going to do about her?"

Even though the lava is still churning inside, I'm already regretting what I said.

"Stop crying," Allie says. She's sitting on the porch steps, half-hidden by a pillar.

"I can't—everything is so awful."

"Yeah, you are."

"*Me?* I mean Dad's deployment."

"And I mean *you*," she says angrily. "You make every single thing about *you*. Dad doesn't *want* to stay there longer! Mom doesn't want him too either. And in case you haven't noticed, he's my dad too."

"I know," I say, shifting my feet uncomfortably.

"No, you don't," she argues. "You think you're the only one who misses him. You think you're the only one with problems."

I tug on the hem of my shirt as Allie's words sink in.

I *do* think I'm the only one who misses him or, at least, the person who misses him the most.

"You're *really* hard to deal with sometimes," Allie continues. "Especially right now."

"I don't mean to be."

"You can't help it, right? Poor, pitiful Ginny, who's just *too smart* for her own good. You need Dad to hold your hand every second."

"I never said that," I mumble.

"Your problem is that you only think about yourself. You're totally self-centered. If you paid attention to what people around you were thinking and feeling, to what *they* wanted, I promise—they'd like you better."

Allie's words are harsh but they ring true. Before I can answer, she gets up and storms off the porch. She grabs her bike from the garage and heads in the direction of the creek.

I watch her go, wishing she and I were mourning Dad's news together, instead of fighting. Wishing she had asked me to go along with her, even though it's clear now that it's my own fault she didn't.

Not a single time have I asked if she was missing Dad too. Not a single time have I said, *Are you okay?*

I was supposed to be the glue—the one holding us together. Instead, I've been the one breaking us apart.

Fact: When two continental plates collide, the earth's crust buckles and folds, forcing up great mountain ranges. The Himalayas and the Alps were formed by this convergence, or coming together.

The next day, I'm sitting alone on the porch swing, feeling too miserable to do anything. I've tried working on a map, reading a book, and doing research for my fact box, but my brain won't cooperate. No matter what I read or look at, all I can think about are the things Allie said to me yesterday.

The front door bangs open, and Allie comes out. She kicks the basket that holds the basketballs and Nerf guns so hard it skids across the porch and down the stairs. One of the basketballs bounces down the walk and out into the street.

Allie doesn't move. She just stares at the ball as it rolls through the cul-de-sac.

"Aren't you going to get it?" I ask her.

Allie jumps. She didn't see me sitting here. "Go away," she mutters.

"*You* go away—I was here first," I snap.

I immediately wish I could take it back. Why are we talking to each other like this?

Allie doesn't take the bait, though. She just stands there, staring out at nothing. I wonder why she's lingering on the porch instead of running over to Rihan's or getting on her bike.

"What's wrong?" I ask.

"Nothing." She pauses. "And...everything."

"Yeah. Me too."

Allie looks at me with an expression I can't quite read. Mistrust? Then she turns on her heel and marches back in the house, letting the storm door slam behind her.

I jump up to follow and find her in the hallway staring at the mudroom hooks. Mom put painter's tape with a name on it over each one.

Allie stands there for a minute, breathing hard. Then she makes a fist, pulls her hand back, and punches the wall beneath Dad's empty hook. The drywall breaks, leaving a hole even bigger than her fist. She immediately cups her wounded hand in her other one, doubling over in pain.

"Allie?!"

I run to the kitchen to get a bag of frozen peas from the freezer. I bring it to her, and she lays it across her knuckles, which are already turning red.

"Should I get Mom?" I ask.

She shakes her head. "She's not here. She ran out to get ink for the printer."

I watch her adjust the peas to cover all four knuckles. "Why'd you do that?" I ask.

"I just felt like punching something," she says, her voice thick.

"You don't punch a wall for no reason," I say, our eyes locking. "Tell me."

She shrugs and doesn't reply. But for once, I can feel her thoughts. Allie and I are like two continental plates, pushing together and buckling in our misery. And without her saying anything, I finally understand that she's as lost without Dad as I am.

I reach over and lift the bag of peas to inspect her knuckles. They look swollen and purple. Of all the stupid things to do.

"Punching the wall was a dumb thing to do," she says, as if reading my mind as well. Her voice hardens. "But you think I'm dumb anyway, don't you? You and Dad, trading all your super-smart facts together. You like leaving me out."

I'm taken aback by the resentment in her voice. I thought she and I had just started to figure out we're on the same side.

"Maybe you're his favorite," Allie says bitterly, "but he's my dad too."

"I'm not his favorite. He doesn't have a favorite!"

Allie snorts. "Yeah, right. You're his genius, magnet-school daughter. Before we moved, he called the principal, the superintendent—*everyone*—to make sure his precious Ginny got into the magnet school here."

"He did?"

Allie nods, and I feel a flutter of gratitude in my heart.

"I didn't know," I say guiltily, thinking of how I told him I hated him.

"Yeah," Allie says. "So before you had your melt-down when he called yesterday, he asked if I'd gotten *my* class schedule yet, and I had to lie because I didn't want to tell him I'm in all the slow classes."

"There aren't *slow* classes." The words leave my mouth before I realize how patronizing I sound.

Allie glares at me. "Do you have any idea what it's like to be your older, dumber sister?"

I don't. But then I don't think she knows what it's like to be her sister either. The one who can't catch a bas-ketball or hang out with a group of kids without trying to teach them something.

"My old school in Fayetteville didn't have tracking," Allie says. "No slow or accelerated classes—they were all the same. I wish we'd stayed. I miss Mara and Avery and all my friends."

This is news to me. She hasn't mentioned Mara for a few weeks. "But you have Rihan and the Stein brothers. You're always hanging out with them!"

Allie blows air through her lips. "Those guys? They're nice, but they're not Mara. She was a real best friend. Until she stopped returning my calls and emails."

"Oh, Allie. I'm sorry." This has happened before when we move—friends promise to keep in touch, but then their lives get busy and the hole we thought we left fills up quickly. I think of all the sleepovers Allie and Mara used to have. They were inseparable. They called themselves *Alliemara*, as if they were one person.

"I hate it here," Allie says passionately, "and I hate Dad for making us move." She lifts the bag of peas off her hand and chucks it at the hole in the wall.

My sister instincts kick in, and I want to tell her that it's not so bad here, that everything will be fine. But I don't believe it myself.

We don't have our dad. And we need him. There's only one thing I can say that might make her feel better.

"I got my school letter too, and even with Dad calling everyone, I didn't get into the magnet. The program's full and they don't have a spot for me."

Allie stares at me, her face unreadable. If she feels badly, she's not showing it. But she's not gloating either.

"So we'll be at the same school this year," she says finally. "Riding the same bus. Grrrrrreat."

"Yeah."

Normally I'd feel hurt by a comment like that. But right now I just feel numb. Nothing seems as important to me as it did before we found out Dad's deployment was extended.

A tear slides down my cheek. Then another. Allie looks away, wiping her own eyes with the back of her hand.

"He won't be here for my birthday," she says. "We'll miss our camping trip."

Dad and Allie go camping, just the two of them, every year for Allie's birthday.

"I'm sorry, Allie."

"He's different when we go camping. We don't talk about school or you or Mom. We just hang out. And he teaches me cool survival stuff. And we make s'mores and eat tons of junk food."

A mean, jealous part of me wonders if Dad has more fun camping with Allie than he does playing fact games with me. But a bigger, nicer part recognizes that Dad's ability to be different for each of us is what makes him such a great dad, and it's why we both need him so much.

"Did you know Mom got rid of our Flat Daddy when we left Tacoma?" I ask.

She nods. "Yeah. I just didn't tell you because I knew you'd be mad."

"Aren't *you* mad?"

"I'm mad about everything."

I want to hug my sister so badly. I wait to see if she moves even an inch toward me, but she seems frozen. So I stay frozen too.

We sit beside each other on the stairs, not talking, until Mom comes home. Then Allie quickly jumps up and hangs a hoodie on Dad's hook to hide the hole in the wall. She jams her hand in her pocket as she breezes past Mom on the way to the TV room.

And just like that—our moment of convergence is over. We're back to being separate plates, slipping and sliding alongside each other.

Fact: The official height of Mount Everest is thirty feet higher than when it was first calculated in 1856. The difference is largely due to how the height is measured and calculated, but scientists believe Everest could be growing one to three feet every three hundred years.

I'm reading in my room when there's a knock on the front door. I ignore it. It's not for me anyway.

A minute later, I hear the knock again, and Mom yells, "Can someone please get that?" Her big deadline is Friday, and she's asked us to stay quiet and go outside as much as possible so she can concentrate.

"I'll get it!" I yell back.

I hurry downstairs, imagining for a split second that it could be Dad. That after our terrible call on Sunday, he immediately quit the army, hopped on a plane, and flew home to us.

When I open the door, I gawk. I'm so surprised, I can't even say hello.

"You okay?" asks Supriya.

I shake off my awkwardness and smile. "Sorry—I thought you were my...I don't know who."

"Oh. Well, do you want to come out?"

"Yeah, sure, okay." I grab my shoes, dropping one in my nervous excitement, then follow her outside.

An eighth grader came over to hang out with me?

We walk down the driveway and stand in the cul-de-sac. Jack and Emily are playing next door with a large plastic truck on a ramp in their front yard, but no one else is around. I have no idea where Allie is.

"What do you want to do?" Supriya asks.

This feels like a test. What I *want* to do is to tell her about Allie punching the wall and my fight with Dad. Or invite her up in my room so I can show her my map collection and see if she wants to make one together. But those are all things about *me*. Allie would say I should think about the other person. Not be "self-centered."

"Play basketball?" I suggest, hoping she'll say no.

"Nah," she says. "I don't really like basketball that much."

Phew—something we have in common. I would feel better if I weren't so worried that I might fail this conversation at any moment and she'll go running home.

I try again. "Allie said there's a creek nearby. We could go there?"

Supriya looks thoughtful. "Maybe later."

I stand, silent and fidgety, hoping she'll make the next suggestion. Then her face brightens, like she has an idea.

"How about if we play a word game?" she says. "I did this at sleepaway camp last summer. One person picks a category, and we go back and forth naming things in that category, and we have to bounce a ball to each other in between. If you miss the catch or can't come up with an answer after three seconds, the other person gets a point."

I won't miss any answers. The ball I might miss, but not any answers.

"Sure," I say. "We've got a rubber ball on our porch."

I run up my steps and grab it from the basket. I follow Supriya out into the center of the court, where we stand about ten feet apart.

"I'll start," Supriya says. "Popular pets."

She does a simple bounce pass to me, which I catch, relieved she doesn't hurl the ball the way Allie usually does. "Cat."

"Dog."

"Hamster."

"Guinea pig."

"Parakeet."

"Fish."

We go back and forth a bunch more until finally Supriya says, "Chimpanzee," and we both laugh.

"You win," she says. "Now it's your turn to pick the category."

I hold the ball, debating what to do. I want to say countries because I know all 195 in the world, and I doubt Supriya does. But I think it'd be a mistake. Pets was a good, neutral category that anyone can do. I should pick something similar. Colors is too boring. Movies is too broad.

For some reason, the ice cream date on the last day of school with Mom and Dad pops into my head. "Ice cream flavors?" I suggest.

Supriya smiles, and I can tell I've made a good choice.

We go back and forth a number of times again, laughing when our answers start to get ridiculous.

After ice cream flavors, we do hobbies, then famous places. I'm able to say some of my favorite geographical sites like the Black Hills, Mount Rushmore, and Yellowstone National Park, while Supriya says things like Radio City Music Hall and Disneyland.

It's Supriya's turn to pick our next category when I see Allie coming up the road on her bike. She's by herself, and her face is stormy.

Allie sees the two of us standing in the court with the ball and sails right by us without a word, parking her bike in the garage.

"Do you want to ask your sister to play?" Supriya asks.

I don't. I'm enjoying hanging out with Supriya alone. It would be a nice thing to do, though. I would want her to ask me if the situation were reversed.

Convergence.

I call out, "Allie, come play Categories with us."

She waits a beat, then answers, "Sounds boring."

"How do you know it's boring unless you try it?" I say, surprised by how much I sound like Dad when he's convincing me to try something new.

Allie stays quiet, either thinking it over or deciding how meanly she can say no in front of Supriya without looking like a jerk.

I keep going, using another of Dad's lines. "If you don't like it, you don't have to keep doing it."

Allie knows what I'm doing and rolls her eyes. But to my surprise, she saunters down the driveway toward us, her ponytail swinging behind her.

"I'll play if I can pick the next category," she says. In agreement, Supriya tosses her the ball.

"Sports without a ball," Allie says, zinging the ball at me.

I catch it, but barely. My brain is churning, trying to think of an answer. All sports have a ball! Don't they? Finally, after a lot more than three seconds, I remember the Olympics.

"Skiing!" I say, passing to Supriya.

"Toboggan."

"Swimming."

"Diving."

"Track."

We go back and forth, back and forth. Allie ends up winning with sailing. It's somewhat easier with three people because you have more time to think of your next answer, but it's also harder because there are two other people who might say it before you do.

"Great category," Supriya says appreciatively.

Allie smiles her real smile, not a fake one. She's having fun.

From behind me I hear, "Can I play?"

It's Kayla.

"Sure." I quickly explain the rules, and Kayla joins in. Her first category pick is famous artists. After the obvious ones like Picasso, Van Gogh, and Georgia O'Keeffe, the rest of us have a hard time coming up with answers.

Not surprisingly, Kayla wins. But no one minds because the game is even better with four people. Everyone has started bouncing the ball harder and faster and shouting their answers.

On my next turn to name the category, I hesitate. Everyone else has picked things they know about, so why shouldn't I?

In my head, I hear Dad saying, *Follow where your compass is pointing, Ginny, not anyone else's.*

"Countries."

Allie rolls her eyes again but keeps her mouth shut, and it ends up being a really good category. Allie gets out first, then Kayla, then it's just me and Supriya. I win with

Vatican City, which is the smallest country in the world, at only 109 acres, or an eighth of the size of Central Park in New York City. It's home to the Pope and located within the country of Italy.

Our game is getting louder and harder when Supriya's dad's car pulls up and Rihan hops out. He comes over and joins us too.

After one round with five players, Allie says, "There's too much time to think of an answer now that there are five of us. Why don't we pass the ball randomly instead of in order? And whoever receives it has to answer."

"Yeah!" agrees Rihan. "That way you always have to have an answer ready."

That's a significant change to the game. It'll be twice as hard because I won't know when the ball is coming at me.

Feeling uneasy, I nod my agreement. I'm doing well thinking up answers, so I focus most of my attention on watching the ball. The categories get more and more interesting, like board games, musical instruments, and languages. I miss the catch a few times, but the game is moving so fast that my fumbles don't stand out. We've reset the score to zero every time a new person has joined and right now I'm in third place. Not the top, not the bottom.

When Lucia comes out later and starts playing, we change the rules again, allowing her to partner with someone. It's her job to catch the ball while her partner answers the question.

Lucia and I are partnered up for vegetables. I've just said rutabaga, which made her laugh, when she says, "I love this, Ginny! I'm glad we're doing your camp again."

"We're not," I say. "This is just..."

My voice trails off as I look around the circle at everyone playing the game together. This *is* like the camp I wanted to create, only better. Because everyone wants to be here, and everyone is pointing it a little bit in their own direction.

26

Fact: In 1916, 1940, and 1944 there were no Olympic Games due to the two world wars. In the ancient Greek Olympics, all wars in the region had to have a cease-fire during the games.

I wake up with the perfect idea for an "I'm sorry I was a jerk" gift for Dad. Once I'm up and dressed, I take a fresh posterboard and my art supplies out onto the front porch. I'm going to make a different kind of map this time, and I hope it'll turn out the way I want it to.

After I've been working for an hour or so, Allie comes outside. Her sneakers are by the front door and she slips them on, probably planning to head to Rihan's.

But instead of running off, she comes over to see what I'm making.

"It's for Dad," I tell her.

She nods. "He'll like it." She's quiet for a minute and I expect her to just walk away, but she continues to stand over me.

She doesn't say anything, and I feel the urge to fill the silence between us. But I force myself to be patient and let Allie speak first.

"I'm going to Rihan's," she says finally. "Wanna come?"

I hold my breath. My sister is inviting me to hang out with her?

"Are you asking me because I told you about my school situation?"

"What does it matter why I'm asking? Just come."

A list of reasons to say no run through my mind. My failed camp. How I overreacted when she Super-Drenched my cards. My awkward attempts to talk to Kayla. But yesterday's success with the categories game makes me wonder if I should try hanging out with the kids in the neighborhood again. I'll be going to school with them soon. With Allie beside me, maybe I can do it.

"What if I get all 'Genius Ginny' and screw something up again?" I ask. "Then everyone will hate me."

Allie's face flushes. "I'm sorry I didn't help you more with your camp. I promised Dad I'd look out for you.

But then I was so miserable, I sort of took it out on you instead."

"It's okay," I say, even though it isn't.

"Listen," Allie says. "You're not as awkward as you think you are. You just get in your own head too much."

"What about my fact-attacks?"

She laughs. "Oh yeah—those." Allie sighs an enormous sigh. "They are annoying. To *me*. But that's also because I don't know what you're talking about half the time. Just...forget everything I said. Forget everything that dumb kid Joey Bingle ever said to you. You're a fact nerd—embrace it. If kids don't like you, then who cares?"

Allie is literally saying the opposite of everything she's ever said to me before. If this were one of the sci-fi movies she and Mom like to watch, this would be the part where I get suspicious and rip off her face to find a robot beneath.

"It's easy for you to say *who cares* because everyone always likes you," I tell her.

She scrunches her nose. "Superficially, maybe. I can make fast friends, but not necessarily good friends."

I think of Mara and how much it must hurt that she isn't replying to Allie's messages.

"Enough talking," Allie says. "Let's round everybody up."

"I'm going to screw it up...."

"If you do something weird or clumsy or whatever, laugh at yourself."

"That's it? Just laugh?"

"Yeah—don't take yourself too seriously. You're not Marie Curie. Yet."

I shake my head. "I want to be like Marie *Tharp*, the cartographer, not Marie Curie. Although Marie Curie was pretty amazing too. She discovered two radioactive elements."

Allie grins. "There's our girl! I said that on purpose."

"No, you didn't."

"You're right—I didn't. I have no idea who you're talking about. C'mon, let's go."

I follow Allie as she gathers up Kayla and her younger brother, Jerome, Lucia, Supriya, and Rihan.

When we're all standing around in the middle of the court, Kayla asks, "So, what are we doing?"

"How about a foul shot contest?" Allie suggests, spinning her basketball on one finger.

"I want to have a cartwheel contest," says Lucia. "Who can do the most in a row."

"I know a fun game," Kayla says. "It's like Telephone except you draw a picture and pass it around, and each person has to copy the picture after looking at it for just fifteen seconds. Then you compare the final picture to the original one."

Her brother, Jerome, who looks about nine, says, "Boooooorrrrring. Let's do street hockey."

"Well, *I* think we should play Zombies in the Graveyard," Rihan says. "And for once we have enough people for a really good game."

Everyone looks at me. Are they waiting for a suggestion, or for me to vote on theirs? Or do they expect me to ruin everything by saying something like *Let's play Geography Hangman*?

I am too in my head, like Allie said. I should just be myself. What do *I* want to do?

And then I get an idea.

"How about we do a Curtis Court Olympics?" I suggest. "That way we can do all the things everyone mentioned. We could have teams, and team names...."

"That's a great idea!" says Kayla.

"Let's do it," says Rihan.

I look around. Everyone is smiling and nodding. They like my idea.

"Allie," I say, "you could be in charge of the shooting contest. If you want."

Allie does a quick dribble between her legs with the ball. "Sure."

"Can you lift me up so I can shoot?" Lucia asks her.

"Yep. And I'll show you a trick to make you jump higher too."

Lucia beams. "Cool!"

I am going to be pretty bad at most of the events, but I don't care. I'm so overjoyed everyone likes my idea that I say, "Did you all know that the athletes in the ancient Greek Olympics competed naked?"

There's a moment of silence as I realize I just quoted a fact. It wasn't a geography fact, but still.

Luckily, Supriya saves me by laughing. "Eww! I did *not* know that, and I don't want to picture it either."

Lucia giggles, and so does Jerome. Pretty soon everyone is laughing and making jokes about doing cartwheels naked.

"Ladies and gentlemen, please line up for the first event," says Rihan, using an announcer voice. "Shooting contest!"

Allie leads us over to the basketball hoop and spends two minutes giving everyone tips on where to place their hands on the ball and where to train their eyes when shooting.

Even with the lesson, I make zero baskets. So does Lucia. Oh well.

Allie ends up winning the contest, of course, making eighteen baskets from a line Rihan draws on the street with chalk. Kayla watches Allie with something like awe. Allie jumps and lands so lightly and deftly on her feet, it makes me think of Dad's nickname for her—Allie Cat. Now I understand where it came from.

"Nice job," I tell her.

Allie shrugs nonchalantly, but I can tell she's pleased. I don't usually compliment her on her athletic ability because I always figured she knew she was awesome.

Next up is the cartwheel contest, which Lucia wins handily, by being able to cartwheel completely around the perimeter of the court without even pausing. I think she does about twenty-five cartwheels, one after the other. I can't believe she doesn't throw up.

I only manage to do three in a row before I fall over. It's a lot harder than it looks. Kayla gets six, and Supriya also has three. Rihan, surprisingly, does twelve, and Allie does fifteen.

Then we try Kayla's version of Telephone. She brings a

notepad and passes out sheets of paper. She starts the game, and everyone takes a turn drawing what they remember from staring at the picture drawn by the person next to them for fifteen seconds. By the end, her original picture of a clown has turned into a witch. It's pretty funny.

I draw the United States Capitol, one of the most recognizable buildings in the country. By the time it gets around the group, it looks like a tree house. No one guesses it correctly so I get a point.

Next, Rihan gathers everyone by the honeysuckle bush in his yard to explain the rules of Zombies in the Graveyard. Even though I don't have many points overall, I don't care. Everyone is bad at one of these games at least. Also, some of them are so ridiculous that it doesn't seem to matter whether you win or lose.

"Earth to Ginny," Rihan says, interrupting my thoughts. "Do you have all that?"

I blink. I completely tuned out during the rules of his game. All I heard was "Earth to Ginny."

I immediately panic, saying, "Did you know Earth is believed to be about 4.5 *billion* years old?"

I close my eyes, frustrated with myself. But Rihan just says, "Uh, no, I didn't know that. And it won't save you from a super zombie. Better run!"

Everyone quickly scatters in different directions, and I end up tailing Kayla behind Lucia's mom's car.

"Go hide somewhere else!" she whispers. "Or we'll both get caught."

"Where should I go?"

"I'm going to run for the bushes by Jack and Emily's house. You run the other direction, okay? Jerome's coming and he's really fast."

"What? Where do I—"

"Just keep moving!" Kayla whispers as she takes off.

I squat behind the tire for another minute, thinking. That's what Mom always tells me—keep busy and keep moving. Maybe she's been right all along.

Fact: Over twenty-five thousand workers died during the construction of the Panama Canal, a fifty-one-mile-long waterway that cuts through the country of Panama and connects the deep waters of the Atlantic and the Pacific Oceans. Most of the deaths were due to yellow fever and malaria.

The next morning, I'm at the table eating a stale piece of toast. We're out of our usual bagels. And orange juice. And even butter.

Allie strolls in and heads to the pantry. She bangs around in the cupboard for a minute before saying, "No bagels?"

"No good cereal either," I say. "Or eggs."

She grimaces. "Mom needs to go to the store."

"I know. But her project is due in two days."

Allie does a few laps around the kitchen, as if expecting good food to magically appear, before finally grabbing the stale loaf of bread and some jelly.

I clear my throat a few times. It feels like crust is caught in there, so I take a sip of water. I miss the tanginess of orange juice.

The toaster dings, and Allie pulls out her toast. The knuckles on her right hand are now a greenish yellow.

"Your hand still looks pretty bad," I tell her.

"Yeah. It feels better, though. Thanks for not telling Mom."

"She's going to notice eventually. Or see the hole in the wall."

"I know," Allie says. "I emailed Dad to ask him how I should handle it."

She plops down opposite me at the breakfast table. Sitting there in the quiet together, I get the same feeling of convergence I did the other day. Even though we're different, Allie and I both need our dad to help us fix whatever problems we're having.

What would Dad do to help if he were here right now? How would he get us through the next seven and a half months?

"The bread's stale," Allie grumbles, getting up to throw her toast in the trash. "And I'm *starving*. We need food. Should I ask Mom to go to the store?"

"You can't—she said not to interrupt her."

And then I get an idea.

When we were little and our rooms were a mess, Dad would stand in the hallway and yell, "Inspection in ten minutes!" And Allie and I would hurry up and clean and make our beds. It felt like a game because at the end we'd have to stand at attention while he inspected each room. And sometimes he'd poke us in the stomach to try and make us laugh.

"The whole house is a mess," I say. "Mom's been working so much that she hasn't had time to do anything. And we haven't been helping. What would Dad say if he walked in the door right now and saw the baskets of dirty laundry in the hall, or the dishes in the sink?"

"He'd be pretty mad at us," Allie replies. "The floor under this table is crunchy."

"So let's clean it up."

"You and me?"

Allie hates chores. In Fayetteville, she usually got out of them by disappearing outside and not returning home until someone else had gotten fed up and done them for her.

"Inspection in ten minutes," I say, making my voice sound like Dad's.

Allie smiles. "I remember that." She's quiet for a moment, then says, "You're right—let's clean up. Dad would want us to.

"*You're* mopping, though," she adds. "I hate mopping."

"Deal," I say, feeling a glimmer of hope. I used to think we were the Atlantic and Pacific Oceans, irreconcilably separated by the country of Panama before the canal was built. But maybe we're not. Maybe we just need to give each other a chance.

I assign myself mopping, vacuuming, and dusting, and Allie gets laundry, dishes, and putting away whatever needs putting away.

I don't know how to mop because I've never done it before, so I end up making the floors look even dirtier than they were until I figure out how the squeezy wringer at the end works.

Allie moves around me, folding afghans and stacking mail and putting away shoes.

Something starts to happen as we're cleaning. Maybe it's because we're working together, but the better the house starts to look, the better I feel. Allie too. She even starts whistling. We spend an hour on the first floor and get it to where it looks almost like it did when we first moved in.

Allie gathers the laundry—whites and colors—and throws it all in together, which I know you're not supposed to do, but I don't say anything. She also drops a bowl while trying to put it away in a high spot and it breaks.

"Do you think Mom'll notice?" she asks me. What she's really asking is, *Are you going to tell on me?*

Maybe a few days ago I would have. Not now.

"She won't notice," I say. "Just sweep the pieces in the trash."

Looking relieved, Allie cleans up the broken bits. Then we stop to survey our work. The house looks so much better.

"Should we make our beds and clean up our rooms?" she asks.

My room is already pretty clean, but I nod anyway. Why stop now? When I finish, I come back downstairs and find Allie on the tablet.

"Are you trying to call Dad?" I ask her, hoping the answer is yes. I want to see his face. I want to tell him how sorry I am for everything I said the other day and that I didn't mean any of it. But I've felt too ashamed to call or email him myself.

"No, I'm ordering groceries," Allie replies. "I saw this service on a commercial, and they deliver from your local store. So I just put in our zip code, and now I'm getting us a bunch of stuff."

I'm impressed. "Great idea!"

Allie doesn't say anything, but I can tell she's pleased with herself.

When the website asks for payment, Allie grabs Mom's purse off the hook in the hallway and digs around in it for a credit card.

"Won't she be mad we didn't ask her first?" I say.

"No, she'll be happy we have food. I think. Plus, I got us frozen pizzas to make for dinner tonight."

Allie is full of good ideas. I wouldn't have thought of any of this.

"I also ordered us some Twizzlers and cheese popcorn," she says, grinning.

Allie is inspiring me. I grab the notepad Mom keeps on the counter and write *Weekly Chores List* at the top. I start dividing up the chores around the house between Mom, Allie, and me. Now that I'm thinking about it, it's pretty crummy that there are three people in this house, yet neither Allie nor I have helped Mom with a single thing since we moved here. Dad would have made sure we were loading the dishwasher and taking the trash out.

When I'm done, I post the new chart on the fridge.

On a fresh page of the notepad, I start doodling a map of Afghanistan, inking the major cities, geographical features, and air bases from memory.

Allie sees my drawing. "What's that?"

I tell her, describing Bagram Airfield and where I think Dad's CSH is, and how they transport the pieces of it across the country by aircraft and truck and set it up.

"How do you know all that?" she asks.

"I've been watching videos online. Too many videos, probably."

Allie's face clouds over. "I try not to think of him being all the way over there," she says. "Even though I know that's where he is. I just think of him as being 'away.'"

"Does it help?" I ask.

She shrugs. "Not really."

She looks so miserable I almost can't take it. Now I understand what Mom meant when she said watching me miss Dad was worse than missing him herself.

I put my pencil down and clap my hands together.

"New category!" I announce. "This time we'll play without a ball."

"What do you mean? We're not playing anything."

"*New category*," I repeat. "Things we miss about Dad."

Allie looks at me, skeptical, her eyebrows raised. I think she's going to tell me I'm being ridiculous, but instead, she says, "Shooting hoops together."

"Sunday pancakes."

"Dumb jokes."

"Sharing new facts."

"Long bike rides."

"Listening to talk radio."

"Driving me to games and practices."

"His hard hugs."

Allie sighs. "Same."

Surprised, I say, "I thought he just did that for me!"

Dad had given me my first big, hard, bear hug when I was about four, after I woke up from a bad dream and couldn't get back to sleep. He'd said he was going to squeeze the bad dream out of me. I thought it was our private joke. All of his hugs afterward were always bear-huggy too.

"It's not just for you," Allie says. "He hugs super-hard to show us how much he loves us."

"Oh," I say, wondering if that could be right. Maybe I saw everything the way I wanted to see it.

With Dad, and with Allie.

⫸———⫷

Later that afternoon, after the groceries have arrived and Allie and I have put them away, Mom calls me into the kitchen.

She's standing by the fridge, pointing to the weekly chore chart.

"Did you make this?" she asks.

I nod.

"And did you clean up the entire house and magically get us food?"

"Allie got the food and did the laundry and dishes. I did the other stuff."

Mom smiles and shakes her head. "You amaze me, Ginny. Your camp gets canceled, you decide to run your own. *That* camp doesn't work, you go back to the one you hated and stick it out. Your mom can't take care of you properly, you step up and take care of her."

I hear the guilt in her voice and feel terrible. "You do take care of me," I tell her. "Allie and I just thought we should help more."

Mom looks sheepish. "Well, whatever the reason, I appreciate it. I know I'm not your father, and that you really need him—"

"I need you too."

She puts her arm around me and squeezes. "Thanks for saying that." We hug for a minute, and then she pulls back and looks at me thoughtfully. "You know, before Dad left, I talked to him about how I could make this move easier on you. But he said you were the ultimate problem solver and that you'd figure it out on your own. I guess he was right."

"Dad said that?"

She nods.

I let that sink in. Problem solvers deal with whatever comes their way. Problem solvers don't wait for circumstances to change, they get busy fixing what they can fix. Problem solvers don't let their family fall apart when they can do something to help.

A problem solver is a pretty good thing to be.

"You were right too, Mom. About a bunch of stuff. Like the Would You Rather game. And going back to jewelry camp."

"Maybe I know you a little better than you think I do."

She does. I thought only Dad knew me, but I was wrong.

"I'm so glad I have you and your sister here," she says. "I couldn't get through Dad being gone without you girls."

"I'm glad we're here too."

"Even Allie?"

"*Especially* Allie. She ordered frozen pizzas for dinner tonight."

Mom's eyes light up. "That sounds delicious. Should I make a salad so we can pretend we're eating a well-rounded meal?"

"Nah. Let's just eat pizza and watch a movie. Your choice. Even one of those terrible zombie apocalypse things you and Allie like."

Mom looks completely taken aback. "I don't know what's going on with you, but I like it."

"Nothing's going on. I'm just in the mood for a family movie night."

Mom smiles. "Me too. In fact, there's nothing I'd like more."

Fact: There are only three countries in the world that don't use the metric system: Liberia, Myanmar, and the United States of America.

Sunday night after dinner, the whole neighborhood is outside playing kickball in the court. Supriya isn't here, but everyone else is.

Allie is pitcher and rolls the ball to me. I kick it—a weak kick, more of an accidental bunt—and head for first base. Allie scrambles forward to get the ball, but I've already landed safely on first base, yelling "Egypt!" as I do.

The other day we were all playing kickball, and just for fun, I started yelling out a country name every time I got on base. At first, I was the only one doing it. But pretty soon Kayla and Supriya started doing it too, then Lucia, who always yells "Canada!" Even the Steins joined in, once they realized they could make it another way to get someone out. They added the rule that if a runner makes it to base but doesn't call out a country that hasn't been named yet, they're out. Allie likes it so much that last night she went online and started memorizing a bunch of countries.

Autumn, the girl who was at horse camp, is back, and she and Kayla's brother, Jerome, are fast runners and know a decent amount of countries. They're both going into fourth grade. Jerome knows more countries than Autumn, probably because of the huge map in his family's kitchen.

Anyway, with Autumn and Jerome, plus Supriya and the Stein brothers, there are sometimes ten kids outside— twelve if little Jack and Emily come out and play.

Allie and I have never lived in a neighborhood like this where the houses are so close and all the kids play together. There's always something to do.

"Look alive, Ginny!" Rihan calls. He's on first base, and I'm on third. Kayla is up at the plate. If she kicks it hard, she might be able to bring us both home, and we'll beat Allie's team.

Allie tries to intimidate Kayla with a fake-out throw, then rolls the ball to her normally. Kayla winds up and makes a huge kick. I run for home, shouting "Brunei!" Rihan follows me with "Japan!" Kayla ends up on second base, with "Norway!"

"We're up six-three!" Rihan says, rubbing it in Allie's face.

"Not for long," Allie replies. "Because Ginny's up next, and if all she has is a bunt, I'm ready for it."

A bunt *is* all I have, so I'll need to run really fast. As I take my place at home plate, my watch buzzes on my wrist. I set the alarm for 7:53 PM. Dad emailed us yesterday and said he was going to call tonight at 8:00 PM, Eastern Daylight Time. It'll be 4:30 AM his time, but he said that's when he has to get up.

I haven't talked to him since the Very Bad Call, and I'm nervous. I've never been nervous to talk to my own father before.

"I've got to go in!" I announce, pointing at my watch as I jog toward our front door.

"You can't leave now!" Kayla moans. "Wait two minutes and take your turn."

"Our dad is calling," I hear Allie explain.

She'll get time alone with Dad too. She and Mom and I talked about it, and we came up with a schedule where we rotate who goes first. Tonight is my turn.

Inside, I find the tablet I left charging on the kitchen counter. I set it up so it's leaning against the utensils jar, and make sure it's fully powered. Then I run upstairs to retrieve the special map I've been working on. How do I explain it to him?

And what do I say when he calls?

There's so much pressure to make every second count. I should probably start keeping a list of things I want to tell him, like Mom does. Hers is on the fridge and it looks like it's written in code, because I don't know what most of the things mean: *The Trelawneys. Jeff's new job. Beach next summer? Chocolate pie. Blue hydrangeas. Vampire book?*

My list would read something like: *New friends. Regular school? Cooking a lot. Nightmares from zombie movie.*

Mom drifts in from the TV room holding a magazine and an iced tea. Since she handed in her big project Friday, she's been less frantic.

"Getting ready?" she asks.

"Yes, it's almost time."

Mom nods. "I'll be out on the porch if you need me. Remember our plan—you, then Allie, then me, then a group goodbye. And we rotate for the next call."

"Uh-huh." I barely hear her. All I can think about is how badly I want to apologize to Dad.

I sit down and stare at my watch until it says 8:00 PM. Any second now.

8:01 PM.

8:02 PM. Did something happen and he can't call?

8:03 PM. *Riiiiiiinng!*

I hit the green button to answer, and there's Dad, his hair rumpled from sleep. He has his glasses on and the terrible mustache is gone.

This is the dad I know. The relief of seeing his familiar face makes me forget my nerves.

"DAD!" I yell. "It's you!"

He laughs. "It's me. Tell me everything about your week. Better or worse than the last one?"

"Better," I say. "But Dad?"

"Yeah?"

I clench both hands into fists beneath the counter where he won't see them. "I'm so sorry about everything I said last time. I didn't mean any of it."

"It's okay, Ginny. I know that."

"I love you," I say quickly. "And I'm so sad you're not going to be back until March, but I know it's not your fault. And I know the school thing isn't your fault either. Allie told me you tried really hard to get me in."

"She told you that?"

"We've been talking more. And hanging out some too."

Dad smiles. "Well. Isn't that something."

"Yeah. We've been playing games outside with the kids on the street. Oh, and Mom just signed me up for a drawing camp! This girl here, Kayla, told me about it and she's a great artist and said it was really good. I thought it would help me improve my map skills."

"Drawing camp? That sounds excellent. Will you draw me a picture of you that I can hang on my wall here?"

"Yes, but it won't be any good."

"I don't care if it's good," he says. "Just that you made it."

"Okay," I agree. "How many more minutes until it's Allie's turn?"

"About four," he says. "Tell me more. How are you feeling about school?"

"Fine—I'm trying not to think about it." The truth is, the thought of going to regular school still makes my knees shake, like a 5.6 tremor on the Richter scale of earthquake measurement.

"Follow your true north, Ginny, and you'll always end up in the right place," Dad says.

There it is again—true north.

"I've been trying to figure out what you meant by that, Dad. At first, I thought it was working toward being a geoscientist so I can make a great discovery."

"Yes, well, that's certainly your passion—"

I cut him off. "But that wasn't it. Then I thought it was just being *myself*. But now I think it's much more than that—now I think that maybe *you* are my true north. And Mom and Allie too. Because without all of you, I could never be happy, no matter where I was, or what I was doing."

Dad blinks hard and clears his throat. "Well, in that case, you're mine too, Ginny. You and your mom and your sister. Home is all I think about, and the only place I want to be."

I don't answer. We stare at each other for a long moment, separated by computer screens and thousands of miles.

"It's going to be seven very long months without you," I whisper.

"Yes, it is," Dad says. "But here's what we're going to do—we're going to set up a weekly Dad and Ginny video date on Sunday nights. And I'm going to find the best Wi-Fi spots here and do *everything I can* to be in one at that time so we can see each other, okay? And then during the week, just email me whenever you can about anything you want. What you had for breakfast. What you're reading. What new fact you've discovered that I can impress my colleagues with here. Just be yourself."

"Really? Anything? I can tell you honestly when I'm grumpy and miserable? I don't have to be all fake-cheerful and perfect?"

"Of course not. I always want you to be honest. And I'll write back as soon as I can, even though it might not be that same day. I can read them all and catch up, so when we talk, I'll know what's been going on with you."

Weekly video chats and emails, when available. I try to look pleased, but Dad can see that I'm forcing it.

"Don't let perfect be the enemy of good," Dad says.

I smile. "Mom told me the same thing."

"I know video chat and email aren't enough, Ginny, but it'll have to do for now."

I nod.

There's a shout from outside. Any second now, Allie will come in for her turn.

"How much time do I have left?" I ask.

"About a minute."

I don't know if I should show him what I made or wait

until our next call when I have more time. I decide to go for it. I pull out the map and hold it up so he can see it.

"What is this?" he says. "It looks like a street map."

I hold it closer to the camera. "Our new street, Curtis Court. I've drawn all the houses, and written who lives in them, and also a bunch of interesting landmarks, like the basketball hoop, the zombie hideout/honeysuckle bush in Rihan's yard, the big globe rock at the end of our driveway, the spot where Kayla paints. Stuff like that. I'm going to keep adding to it. That way, when you come back..."

I pause, my throat immediately thick. I take a second to clear it.

"When you come back in March," I try again, "you'll know the lay of the land, and you can feel right at home here."

Dad smiles, and his eyes look almost teary. "Now *that* is a great map, Ginny."

Allie bursts into the house then, running straight for me and the tablet. "Is it my turn yet?" she asks.

"Is that my Allie Cat?" says Dad. And that's it—my private time is over. It was practically a blink.

I pass the tablet to Allie, feeling a mix of relief and sadness from the too-fast chat.

"Thanks," she says to me. "Dad! I've got so much to tell you. I've been working on my 'nothing but net' shots..."

As Allie launches into a story, I realize I didn't even get the chance to ask Dad any questions about him. I just talked about myself the whole time. I whip out an index card from my pocket and write, *Ask Dad to tell me three interesting things he's doing* for our video date next week.

As Dad said, it isn't perfect, but it's better than nothing.

I want to hang out and stand behind Allie as she talks so I can at least look at Dad's face and hear his voice for a bit longer, but the three of us agreed in advance to give each other time alone with him. So I go out on the porch and sit down on the swing. Mom is over in Lucia's yard, talking to her mother.

After a minute, Mom joins me on the porch. She checks her watch and points toward the door. "Is it my turn yet?"

"I think Allie has another minute or two. Dad has less time than he thought so we each get seven minutes. The whole thing is kind of a mess."

"I agree," Mom says. "Although, when you think about it, some of our happiest times together started out as a mess."

That's true. I remember one vacation where we were driving five or six hours to go to the beach, and Allie and I both got the stomach flu. We threw up in the car the entire way there. But when we finally arrived, we both felt better and ended up having the best week ever.

"Would You Rather have a life filled with travel, adventure, and *mess*, or the same old thing all the time?" Mom asks. "I know my answer."

She kisses my forehead and goes inside to wait for her turn. I stay on the porch and watch the sun go down. It's to my left, which means our new house faces north. True north—the one where the lines of longitude converge.

Maybe it's a sign I'm in the right place after all.

Fact: About fifty animal species, including birds, mammals, reptiles, and insects, use the earth's magnetic field for navigation. Even desert ants use it to find their way back to the nest.

The next Sunday, Mom and I are making tacos for dinner. She shows me how to brown the ground beef, and while it's cooking, I start putting toppings in bowls.

Dad is planning to call us at eight o'clock again. I have a list in my pocket of things to ask him and things to tell him so that I don't waste any of my time.

Allie has already set the table and is outside finishing up a game of basketball with Rihan and Jerome. Lucia is playing too. When she wants to shoot, Allie holds her up in the air. Allie says Lucia has "good hustle."

"Are you excited about tomorrow?" Mom asks, reaching around me to get the taco seasoning from the pantry.

Tomorrow is the first day of the drawing camp that Kayla told me about. Allie's going to be at basketball camp, so I figured this would be a good week for me to stay busy.

"Yeah, I think it'll be fun. I wish I knew someone else doing it, though."

"Drawing isn't a particularly social activity," Mom says. "So even if you don't find someone to talk to the first day, it won't be awkward."

"That's true. It's not like school."

At the mention of school, Mom looks pained. She knows I'm still worried about going to Greenwood. But I'm starting to feel better about it because at least I'll know the kids on the block and Allie. That's something. Plus, I can always hang out with Supriya after school.

"Watch the meat for a sec," Mom says, heading into the hallway. I hear her open the closet door and rustle around for something.

The beef is sizzling, its edges starting to brown. I turn the heat down slightly. The more I cook, the more I like it. It requires focus and precision, two things I'm good at.

Mom returns, clutching a white plastic bag. She hands it to me. "I got this a few weeks ago and was saving it for a back-to-school present. But I think you might appreciate it now."

Curious, I open the bag and pull out a T-shirt that reads: *Without geography, you are nowhere.*

I look up at her, surprised. "I *love* it!"

"You do?"

"Yes!" I quickly pull the shirt on over top of my other one, carefully smoothing the front so the words aren't bunchy.

"I saw it online, and it made me laugh," Mom says.

Impulsively, I hug her. *Without geography, you are nowhere.* That's exactly how I feel.

And now I know Mom understands.

"I can wash it tonight if you want to wear it for camp," she says. She turns the heat down even lower on the beef and gestures at the green onions for me to chop.

I line up the onion bulbs and begin to slice them, making sure to keep the tip of my knife on the board the way Mom showed me. Even though I love the shirt, I'm not sure I want to wear it to camp tomorrow.

I finish the green onions and sweep them from the cutting board into a bowl, thinking about how some people don't like onions. My dad loves them. I do too.

We are who we are. We like what we like.

"Thanks, Mom," I say. "I think I will wear it tomorrow. But you don't have to wash it—I'll throw in a load after dinner."

Mom smiles as she hands me a tomato to slice. "Sounds good to me."

She calls Allie inside for dinner. As Allie sits down and grabs her napkin, some green onions fall out of it. She shakes it, and even more of them fall on the floor. When Mom picks up her napkin, the same thing happens.

They both look at me, baffled.

"I wonder how those got there?" I say innocently.

Mom and Allie both laugh, and I know we're all thinking about Dad, but in a happy way. And how in less than two hours, we have a call with him.

"Let's eat," Allie says, pulling a piece of gum out of her mouth and sticking it on the edge of her plate. "I'm starving."

Mom frowns. "Put that in the trash first, please."

Allie gets up to throw it out and when she comes back, I say, "Did you know it's illegal to sell chewing gum in Singapore?"

"I did not know that," Mom says. "What else is illegal there?"

"You can also get fined for forgetting to flush a public toilet, spitting in public, or for playing an instrument outside."

"The Stein brothers better not go to Singapore, then," Allie says. "They'd get in a lot of trouble."

I laugh, and Mom shakes her head. "I'm not even going to ask."

When we finish eating, Mom tells us to close our eyes and stay at the table while she clears the plates. Alarmed, Allie and I exchange a look.

"Why do we have to close our eyes?" she asks.

"Is it something bad?" I say.

"Trust your mother," Mom replies. "It's something good."

We close our eyes and don't peek. At least, I don't.

I hear plates clattering and some cabinet doors opening and shutting. Then there are several thuds on the counter. A minute later, Mom yells, "Surprise!"

I open my eyes and see the ingredients to make sundaes lined up on the kitchen counter: two kinds of ice cream, that fancy chocolate sauce that hardens, whipped cream, sprinkles, nuts, and cherries.

Mom never buys junk food like this. "What's the occasion?" I ask.

"The occasion," Mom says, "is that we're going to be having our weekly calls with Dad on Sundays, and it's so hard to wait that final hour before the call. So I thought a sundae bar would give us something to do every week."

"Every week?" Allie says excitedly. "Really?"

Mom nods. "We're deployed too. We deserve a treat, don't you think?"

"Can we call them our Sunday sundaes?" I ask.

Mom says, "Absolutely" at the same time Allie says, "Do we have to?"

"Yes, we have to," I say happily. "Don't worry—it'll grow on you, Allie."

"Yeah, like a fungus," she replies, handing me the ice cream scoop.

I wipe it off with a paper towel and dig into the tub of vanilla. "Speaking of fungus, did you know the largest living organism in the world *isn't* the blue whale, but is actually a fungus that covers about *four square miles* of forest in Oregon?"

"Just scoop your ice cream, Ginny," Allie says.

"They call it the Humongous Fungus. Isn't that awesome?"

Allie doesn't reply as she squeezes chocolate sauce onto her sundae. I poke her stomach with my finger just as the bottle makes a loud, gasping noise, and she laughs.

"Okay, okay," she admits. "I guess a humongous fungus does sound kind of cool."

I smile, satisfied. "It only takes one fact to get hooked, Allie."

"It's going to take a lot more than one for me," she replies.

I just keep smiling. We've got plenty of time.

Scientists say that every couple hundred thousand years or so, the earth's magnetic pole flips. The North Pole becomes the South Pole and vice versa. As a result, the species that rely on the magnetic field to navigate get lost.

Eventually, however, their internal compasses adjust to the polar flip and start pointing them in the right direction again.

Home.

United States Capitals
(because Ginny thinks you should learn them)

1. Alabama—Montgomery
2. Alaska—Juneau
3. Arizona—Phoenix
4. Arkansas—Little Rock
5. California—Sacramento
6. Colorado—Denver
7. Connecticut—Hartford
8. Delaware—Dover
9. Florida—Tallahassee
10. Georgia—Atlanta
11. Hawaii—Honolulu
12. Idaho—Boise
13. Illinois—Springfield
14. Indiana—Indianapolis
15. Iowa—Des Moines
16. Kansas—Topeka
17. Kentucky—Frankfort
18. Louisiana—Baton Rouge
19. Maine—Augusta
20. Maryland—Annapolis
21. Massachusetts—Boston
22. Michigan—Lansing
23. Minnesota—Saint Paul
24. Mississippi—Jackson
25. Missouri—Jefferson City
26. Montana—Helena
27. Nebraska—Lincoln
28. Nevada—Carson City
29. New Hampshire—Concord
30. New Jersey—Trenton
31. New Mexico—Santa Fe
32. New York—Albany
33. North Carolina—Raleigh
34. North Dakota—Bismarck
35. Ohio—Columbus
36. Oklahoma—Oklahoma City
37. Oregon—Salem
38. Pennsylvania—Harrisburg
39. Rhode Island—Providence
40. South Carolina—Columbia
41. South Dakota—Pierre
42. Tennessee—Nashville
43. Texas—Austin
44. Utah—Salt Lake City
45. Vermont—Montpelier
46. Virginia—Richmond
47. Washington—Olympia
48. West Virginia—Charleston
49. Wisconsin—Madison
50. Wyoming—Cheyenne

Acknowledgments

First and foremost, thank you to my world-class agent, Alex Glass, who saw the potential in this manuscript and helped it find the perfect home with Christy Ottaviano. Christy, you knew exactly where Ginny needed to go and steered me until we got there. Thanks also to the entire team at Little, Brown for their support of this novel and to Kelly Murphy, for the delightful cover and illustrations.

Several military families were kind enough to share their experiences with me and read my manuscript, including Dr. Matt and his family, and Colonel David L. Greenburg, United States Army Medical Corps; Rebecca Ward, PharmD; and their daughters, Lucy and Lily Greenburg. I'd also like to acknowledge the families of government agencies such as the FBI, State Department, USAID, ICE, et cetera, who also move regularly and live with increased risk to ensure the safety of their fellow Americans. Special thanks to Julian Barnes, national security reporter at the *New York Times*, who offered guidance on the war in Afghanistan.

The DC Commission on the Arts and Humanities, which receives funding from the National Endowment for the Arts, awarded me a work-in-progress grant for this book in 2018. Thank you for supporting artists in our nation's capital.

A writer is only as good as her workshop group, and I'm indebted to Pamela Ehrenberg, Kristin Levine, Erica Perl, and Tammar Stein, for the many, many drafts they critiqued. Extra-special thanks to group member Katherine Marsh, the ultimate literary problem solver.

Thank you to Lisa Graff and Lisa Greenwald for twenty years of true-blue friendship, support, and writing retreats. I'd share facts and snacks with you anytime.

Much love to my parents, Paul Sr. and Patricia Smith, who have been my glue, especially during the last few years.

I've never met anyone who followed their own true north as steadfastly as my brother, Paul Smith Jr., whom we lost in 2019 but lives in my heart every day.

Lastly, to my husband, Michael, and our daughters, Bridget and Rory—wherever you are is where I want to be. And that's a fact.